Madame Mephisto

a novel

Madame Mephisto

a novel

by A.M. Bakalar

STORK
PRESS

Published by
Stork Press Ltd
170 Lymington Avenue
London
N22 6JG

www.storkpress.co.uk

First Published 2012
1

Paperback 978-0-9571326-0-3
eBook 978-0-9571326-1-0

Designed and typeset by Mark Stevens in 10.5 on 13 pt Athelas Regular

Printed in the UK by MPG Books Group Ltd

To Mum, Dad, and Asher

From an economic point of view,
a person's decision to enter into the drugs trade as a
producer, distributor or retailer is entirely rational,
because the profit margins are so high.

Misha Glenny - *McMafia, Crime Without Frontiers*

Why should I fear   the things I fear?
Why shouldn't I have fears?

Maryam Huleh - *The Sticky Dream of a Banished Butterfly*

one

URBAN DICTIONARY ON POLAND: A nation that is unaware of its own collective backwardness, to its utter tragedy. It works efficiently only under occupation and dictatorship. Xenophobic and nationalistic.

You don't believe me? It gets better. Have you heard of a country where twin brothers rule, one the president, the other the prime minister? No? How about this one: the president dies in a plane crash, for which he was most probably responsible because he forced the pilot to land, killing himself, his wife, and ninety-four other people? Did I hear you right? You say it's a conspiracy theory? Not so fast.

It is your country we are talking about.

But maybe you are right. It is all fucked up anyway.

I am sorry, perhaps I shouldn't swear. Not in front of you, at least. And we are going to a funeral in five days. But there is still time before we pay our respects.

You see, there are some things you should know about our country. And our family of course since, well, you and I are going to spend lots of time together. And I am not talking about those many hours before the last rites. Everybody is so busy with grieving and lamenting that they almost forget about you. You could say we have a lifetime ahead with each other.

What? Don't look at me like that. There is nothing to be afraid of. You will learn to appreciate me. Oh, for Christ's sake, don't cry now! I am not a monster. But hold that thought. You see, my mother once said to me: 'How can you be my daughter?' A bit harsh, if you ask me, don't you think?

If I were you I would listen to what I have to say in the coming days because I am doing you a favour. I like to think of it as a rescue operation. Oh no, I did not ask for it. Believe me, taking care of you is the last thing I need in my life. I had no choice. Nobody asked for my opinion.

This family! It's so much easier to love each other from a distance.

So here we are now, you and I. We will see about the future later.

Anyway, we may as well spend this time we have together getting to know each other, or you getting to know me. Here in this room, in my parents' house. Did you know that it was built in 1928? Of course not. How would you know? Mind you, it is a very solid construction unlike what they build these days. They moved to this house in the late 1990s from a block of flats we used to live in.

Are you comfortable? Good. I will place a pillow under your head.

Let me make it easier for you and lay down the options. You can listen to what I have to say and make up your own mind about whether you want to leave with me for London after the funeral. Or you can simply ignore it and get on with your life, here in this country I decided to leave a few years ago. But you should know that if you choose to stay I will not be able to help you because the family I left behind don't exactly wish me well, and are not the kind of people I think you should stay with anyway. But we will get to that later.

Why am I saying this? Oh, because I am – well, how to put it? I guess you could call me a herbal purveyor. My clients call me a guardian angel, a lifesaver. Commonly known as a cannabis dealer if you insist on using the, in my opinion, outdated terminology. But this is not the only reason why my family is reluctant to welcome me back.

I am a professional liar. I am two people. I take pleasure in experimenting with people's emotions, people who trust me, putting their understanding of me in doubt.

Basically, I am the best thing that could have happened to you.

You see, I offer you a once in a lifetime chance to change your destiny. Learn from my mistakes. As I said earlier, I did not ask for it but since we have found ourselves in this situation we may as well use it as a business opportunity. Let's say I have acquired enough and I am ready to share. And since I hate surprises I think it would only be fair to show you the whole picture.

As I was saying, I left the country a few years ago. It was 2004, and Poland joined the European Union. I felt no patriotic duty to stay. Living in Poland was a structured phase of my life. I had just spent four years working as a translator in a bank, right after I did my university degree in translation studies. It was a cover job.

You need to have a cover job if you don't want to get caught. This is your first lesson. You should remember that. You see, I did not actually need to leave as I was already making good money, from dealing cannabis, of course, not as a translator. Growing and selling weed made me feel needed, appreciated, rewarded. Simply put, there is no comparison between working in an office and working as a cannabis grower.

After Poland joined the EU we, the young people, had such hopes, hopes for our own country. That things would get better from now on! There's nothing better than being young and naïve, with no imminent danger of future responsibilities like parenthood, marriage, paying taxes – basically being a good citizen. Some call it contributing to society.

Trust me, it's all bullshit.

Do you remember what I said about the twin brothers? Well, it was like the movie they starred in when they were thirteen. What was the title? Ah yes, *The Two Who Stole the Moon*, about two cruel and lazy boys who one day have an idea to steal the moon, which – in the story – is made of gold, so that they will not have to work any more. You see, those twin brothers later became two cruel politicians who, like the boys in the movie, had a vision of the glory of this country. Yes, you are right, unlike the boys in the movie, the brothers did have jobs – president and prime minister – but their paranoid ultra-nationalism and obsessive religiousness has turned our country into a place I can no longer call my home. It is not always about money, so I can't complain. (Mind you, the UK has one of the largest cannabis markets.)

You see, in a way, the twin brothers made it so much easier for me to make this decision and leave. After Poland became a member of the EU I gave up on my homeland and devised a plan to retreat to London.

There was also the question of my family, or my mother to be precise, who I thought would be the main beneficiary of my absence. Don't get impatient. We will get to the family. But first things first.

A cover job. Remember?

When I think about the first few years of my life in London, I admit that I was not ready to circulate amongst the Westerners. You must remember the years of communist propaganda did a good job of temporarily carving its way into my emotional system. Under the banners of the Polish United Workers' Party to the victory of socialism! The Polish–Soviet friendship!

Bollocks.

Perhaps I did not smile as much as was expected of me during my first job interview in London, which unsurprisingly turned out to be a failure. I tried to be friendly and unthreatening.

But smiling was something I had yet to master. No matter how much I wanted to escape from my birthplace, and find solace in inventing my new immigrant identity, I was forced to admit to myself that the essence of my being was formed where I came from. And where you and I come from a smile is a rare phenomenon, perhaps because of the turbulent history of our country, feeding fears and expectations directly to the heart of each Pole. Poles have a talent for lamenting, endlessly dissecting the events of the past.

While I was battling the crowds on Oxford Street, trying to squeeze my way towards the pedestrian crossing, I received a phone call from the little-known agency called Office Beasts that set up my first interview.

'I'm sorry but you didn't get the job.'

'What?' I said against the roaring noise of a double-decker bus passing in front of me.

'It's not that you don't have the right experience. They really liked you. But they said, and please don't feel bad about it, they said you're too beautiful and they would have trouble working with you. We'll find something else for you.'

'Why don't you send me where looks do matter?' I asked, but it was unnecessary. Office Beasts never set up another interview and I didn't know enough about political correctness to question what I had been told.

Of all the insecurities I brought with me – my imperfect command of English with a dominant Polish accent, my unprivileged non-Western education, and my lack of work experience – my face hardly made it to the list.

My first job interview in Poland had not gone well either, in fairness. With a degree in my hands I knocked on the door of the biggest bank. Ah, those were the days of the Celtic Tiger, and the Irish were investing in the Polish banks before anybody else in Western Europe realised that the countries of the former Soviet bloc would soon become goldmines of opportunity. McDonald's had just opened its doors and we all queued for hours to taste the West. The new owners needed translators and interpreters, and I needed a cover job for my budding cannabis enterprise.

The president of the bank, a Polish man in his early sixties, looked at me with curiosity. Or was it my breasts he was staring at? I do not remember exactly.

'When are you planning to get married and have children?' he said.

'I don't.'

He laughed. 'A young and beautiful woman like you will surely find a husband very quickly and we will lose a translator when you get pregnant.'

I came home that day and told my mother that I got a job because my boss liked my face and my breasts. She shrugged. 'What's wrong with that? You got the job,' she said.

I admit my looks helped me in the past, but I did not come to London to face the same judgment.

Lesson number two: don't underestimate your appearance. Learn about the market and your clients. I did not know it then, but in my line of work I can't emphasise it enough. BPR – behaviour pattern recognition: never act as if you are carrying illicit substances. Who do you think the police are going to suspect first as a marijuana dealer: a woman wearing an impeccable suit who works in a well respected company, preferably in the City or Mayfair, or a black guy with the stink of weed about him? That's right! You already have the answer. Image! Façade of trust and honesty. Your biggest asset is the fact you are an attractive woman. Use it! There is more to it than that, but for now that is all the information I am going to give you.

As I said earlier, I was not ready to work among the Westerners. After the first interview in London I cut my long blonde hair, much to my mother's displeasure. According to her, it was throwing away the biggest asset that could make a difference among the possible suitors for my hand. Abnormal, was the word my mother used to describe me, and in the same breath she praised my twin sister's sensibility. Alicja served as an example I should aspire to, with an established career as a corporate lawyer, and long hair accentuating her femininity, of course.

Polish women make good housewives; a two-course dinner is always ready on time, the house is scrubbed clean, the children are taken care of, and at night we transform into sexually insatiable goddesses. Making a career is the last of our worries, because it is the family, husband and children who always come first. Simply put, a Polish woman is one of the best deals on the matrimonial market.

Much to my mother's disappointment, I yearned for a childless and marriage-free existence, whether in Poland or in England, and with the list of expectations relentlessly drummed into my head since I was a child at school and at home, I felt I had to escape my conventional predicted future. I was terrified by the prospect of ending up like my mother; a faithful and devoted housewife. It was not only how she groomed us at home when we were children: weaving ribbons into our plaited hair, buying colourful fabrics on the black market to sew skirts on the Singer sewing machine, knitting pullovers out of pink wool; my childhood was full of my mother's commanding voice: 'Don't splash soup on your blouse'; 'Stop laughing so loud'; 'Sit straight with legs together, you are not in a barn.'

Don't be surprised. My mother is the product of a strict Catholic upbringing. And I can tell you now that if you decide to stay here, she will get her hands on you before you know it.

Unfortunately, it did not end with my mother. At primary school, Alicja and I were taught to bake, knit, and make sandwiches, while the boys built birdhouses, learnt about car engines, and assembled radios. I, too, wanted to build birdhouses. At secondary school, my mother made sure Alicja and I attended classes on religion. Catholic religion – it is not like in the UK where you have a chance to learn about other denominations. Here you will learn only about sweet Jesus.

I say, forget about Jesus. There are so many gods to choose from.

My mother was friends with Father Maciej, who dutifully reported whenever I skipped classes. What she did not know was that I would use the hours of freedom to hang around the park near the secondary school where I smoked my first joint and listen to the Doors on a Polish-made Diora cassette player. It was so much more fun than memorizing the Ten Commandments.

I was popular among the boys. I think for the first time I realised that there was an opportunity for me. I was not only interested in getting stoned in the park but I was already collecting my first list of future contacts. I smoked, I observed, I listened. I sometimes let them fondle my breasts or lifted my skirt to show them my knickers, and in return, they told me who their suppliers were, how much they paid, who their friends were in other schools who also bought ganja. Most importantly I felt safe. The boys, who later became my devoted clients, never thought of me as a potential wife.

Alicja deliberately chose to prove that individuals can change the stereotypes. 'It's up to you,' my sister would say. She was impatient to demonstrate her being a girl had nothing to do with being successful; I was impatient to leave for a place where I did not have to justify myself.

Several interviews later, I eventually got a full-time job at a major diamond company as a junior assistant in the marketing department. Hatton Garden – the perfect environment for a dealer. Did I hear you right? Imagine the possibilities, the rich clients. But at that time I was nobody in London and I knew nobody. I refused to pimp my product on the streets. I still had a lot to learn. The salary was at least six times more than I could make in Poland. I decided to watch and listen. Eventually I would find the right person.

The post-communist hunger struck and I spent most of my salary every month on shoes and handbags, and everything else I did not need. When I came to the UK I was economically starved. I had all this drug money back home but I could not buy the products I wanted. I was greedy to have a surplus of everything in my life. Splashing cash on fancy Western products which my family could hardly afford would have raised suspicions. You must understand that until I decided to leave Poland I still lived with my parents.

Now, there is lesson number three for you. Don't get greedy. The last thing you need is people, especially your family, wondering how you could possibly afford all these expensive things. Best to keep a low profile, especially if you still live with your parents.

I am sorry. I did not mean to upset you. Let's carry on.

I settled into my first job, in the safety of my colleagues' familiar smiles. I did not think that anything unexpected could happen. At the beginning I did not have a reason to develop cautiousness towards the people I worked with. I did not realise what lay beneath the surface of their exaggerated politeness. I let myself trust them because, despite my arousing their curiosity (I was the only Pole working for the company), they accepted and tolerated me. I did not think there were any barriers between us. Why would I? As I walked the corridors of the company, every person welcomed me with a grin and a question: 'Are you settling in well? Are you enjoying yourself?' As if my wellbeing was everybody's personal agenda.

It was the first observation about my new life that I reported to my mother. 'They are hiding something,' she said. 'Nobody smiles unless they want something from you.' I told her she was overreacting.

Occasionally the people I spoke to would display a look of bewilderment when I spoke about our country, its religiousness or cuisine, but I thought my stories were simply too exotic.

'You've got a funny accent,' I heard one day at lunchtime from one of my colleagues when we both stood in the queue in the company's canteen. 'Where are you from?'

'Poland.'

'Really? So you people were like part of Soviet bloc? But now it's safe to travel there, isn't it?'

'No Soviet army on the streets any more.'

'You're so lucky to be in London.' I was rewarded with a sympathetic smile.

I hardly expected them to understand since even I realised how ludicrous my stories must have sounded to them when I heard myself trying to explain the daily hardships of emerging from communist rule. Some English live in blissful ignorance of their superiority, of their well-established democratic ways and equal rights. My presence in their company was proof they were doing the right thing, giving me a chance to experience what I lacked back home.

I had been working for the company for two months now. In the first week of December the management announced a Christmas party. I did not think the people I worked with would treat the whole incident at the party so seriously. I certainly did not. Basically after one too many glasses of champagne, and an ecstasy pill I had swallowed in the ladies' toilet, I joined the table of senior executives and decided to smoke a cigar with them. It did not end there because when I got bored with the conversation I left them and jumped on the stage. My soul woke up to the beat blasted by the DJ the company hired to entertain the younger staff. Below me was a liquid mass of bodies. I must admit, I had encouraged more attention than I intended.

The only good thing that came out of this mess was sex with Percy Jantjes, a South African lawyer, who worked for the company. We got back to his place after the party came to its end around one in the morning.

Still, I broke one of my own rules: don't draw attention to yourself. But if you don't make mistakes you will never learn. A simple truth but a very good one. You should remember that as well.

I was still in the black cab going back home from Jantjes's flat in Notting Hill when I called Alicja. 'You promised you wouldn't do anything stupid,' she said. I failed to convince her in my drunken voice that my disruptive behaviour – the dancing, not the sex – was largely exaggerated and would be quickly forgotten. She had a different opinion. Besides, as far as I remember, I never promised her I wouldn't do anything stupid.

I naïvely thought that the Monica Lewinsky scandal would be forgotten by now. I underestimated the culture I was living in. In different circumstances there would be nothing wrong with a woman smoking a cigar, except I worked for a company with more than one hundred years of tradition and which employed whole generations of families, mostly Oxbridge educated.

Correction – there were some gays who commented with a sorrowful shake of their heads on my misguided colour coordination: 'Darling, if you don't mind me saying, those colours are so yesterday. It's black, black, black.' I went shopping for new clothes, all black of course, the same day.

What attracted Human Resources' attention more than smoking the cigar was the fact that I openly talked to people I was not supposed to. The company I worked for had invisible glass partitions, safely guarding the executives from the lower-level employees.

The culture that looked so welcoming suddenly began to feel very alien.

'There was a complaint against you,' Jantjes told me two weeks later at his place. He was my first link to the cannabis business I was yet to establish in London.

I took a spliff from his hands. 'It's good.'

'Swazi gold.'

'Have you got more of it?'

'I have a small amount of Zimbabwean mbanje and some Malawian chamba. I'm not sure you will like them.'

'Let me try.'

He took a thin long wrap and handed it to me. 'Malawian. It's called a kop or a head.'

I gently rolled the tightly wrapped cob in my fingers. It was small enough to place it in my pocket. He took it from me, cut the wrapping and rolled a spliff with no tobacco.

'Nah, I think I will stick with Swazi gold,' I said after a while, filling my lungs with the chamba smoke.

'Dagga and Swazi gold are most popular. Dagga costs almost nothing in South Africa. Around £22 per kilo, loose leaves, straight from the producer.'

'You're joking,' I said. I quickly made a calculation in my head. The average street price for South African cannabis in the UK was more than £3,700.

'So what's this complaint about?' I asked.

'You are a bad girl, you know that?' he said, biting my ear.

Jantjes blocked my next question with his lips on mine while I kept thinking that the complaint must have been made by somebody who witnessed my behaviour. How was it possible that an immigrant with a dubious command of English could so easily befriend the senior executives? It was a question that probably rattled through the brain of the person who made the complaint. Instead of staying quiet and inconspicuous, within my bounds, I had dared to make myself visible.

I blamed Percy Jantjes. He should have warned me. After all, he often complained about 'certain cultural inconsistencies,' as he put it, that I should be aware of. I remember him cautioning me against some of our colleagues.

'They're not what they seem,' he said. 'And one more thing: maybe it would be better if we were not seen talking with each other in the company, at least until the situation quietens down a bit.'

'I grew up in a police state. I think I can handle a few overzealous Englishmen who have a burning desire to get rid of me,' I said. 'Back to business. Can you get me in touch with somebody on the ground?'

During working hours we began to maintain a professional aloofness. In Jantjes's flat we smoked and fucked. He was attracted to my Slavic side, the distortions in my accent, and he liked it when I spoke Polish to him during sex. 'Say something in your language,' he would ask me. And I recited poems I remembered from my secondary school by the greatest Romantic Polish poets, Mickiewicz, Slowacki, Norwid. When I recall how he got aroused to the words 'For a year I'll make my dwelling with Beelzebub,' I thought that perhaps I should have chosen a different profession. It all came so easily.

In exchange for sex he told me everything he knew about cannabis production in South Africa. Don't make that face at me. I told you, you should use your assets as a woman. Besides I found him equally exotic, with his Afrikaans, which he mostly used for swearing. His parents exchanged their involvement in the anti-apartheid struggle for a vineyard in eastern Stellenbosch. Percy Jantjes knew a grower who cultivated cannabis crops in the KwaZulu-Natal province. He said the money from wine production did not come near the profits on exporting South African weed. 'You are on your own,' Jantjes told me when he handed me a phone number written on a piece of torn newspaper. 'Wait till I introduce your name first before you make contact. Always call him from a different phone number.' He did not want to know the details. He only bought enough for himself and his close friends to smoke but he was not involved in drug trafficking.

I rewarded his trust with more sex.

For the next month I took his advice about keeping my distance so seriously that he finally approached me near the lifts.

'I don't want to be branded as a troublemaker,' I explained.

He made sure nobody was around before he drew me closer to steal a kiss from me.

'It's too late now,' Jantjes said, still holding me his arms.

But I was confused and did not share his laughter. I did not know how to read my colleagues any more. The feeling of security I had developed working in this company for the last six months changed into a form of paranoia. Could they actually get rid of me because of a stupid incident at a Christmas party?

'Don't be silly. Of course not,' he said, but his answer did not sound convincing.

You see, you should always be vigilant and assume the worst-case scenario. I did not. This, I think, is lesson number four. I hope you are keeping count but please stop me if I am wrong.

At the beginning of February, a special edition of the internal newspaper distributed via email to all workers in the company had a picture of me on the front page – my silk skirt lifted above the knee level, my arms thrown up in the air, my lipstick-stained lips around a fat cigar. It was not the image my mother would picture when thinking about her daughter working abroad.

I am glad it makes you smile. It is reassuring to discover that at least one person in this family has a sense of humour.

From now on I did everything I could to keep a low profile, restricting interaction with my colleagues to a bare minimum. I kept telling myself that soon my unfortunate conduct would be forgotten. I limited my visits to the company's canteen, I chose my smoking spots carefully, tucked away in a side street rather than in front of the main entrance, and I used the staircase instead of the lifts to avoid my colleagues' curious glances.

The company gave me one last chance to prove my fading obedience during the selling days held every five weeks. It was Percy Jantjes who pulled a few strings to get me into this. He was thoroughly civil, which I appreciated. Or maybe by then he knew that I was on the way out and it was just a matter of when it would happen. Either way, I was impressed. Not to the point where I would go back to him, but I did thank him for using his influence. 'Everyone deserves a second chance,' he said to me in his office and I attributed his comment more to his good nature than to the fact that I was still upset he was somewhat ashamed to be seen talking to me.

The diamond selling days were a party of precious stone indulgence, hosted for the exclusive and highly esteemed diamond traders, known as the sightholders. Each sightholder would enter an empty room, empty, that is, except for a dark cloth-bound table where the diamonds were later displayed. In case anybody had the audacity to launch an attack from the opposite building and steal the rocks straight from the table, the windows were bulletproof. I know because I checked – one of the advantages that comes from smoking weed with the lawyer, who knows the secrets of the company.

Who could be better at the diamond trade than Orthodox Jews? As expected, they arrived in large numbers. Because I was a woman, but not one of their wives, I was instructed not to engage in any kind of conversation with the Orthodox Jewish diamond traders. God forbid I was menstruating! I wondered if Jantjes's favour was nothing but a bad joke.

'Do I actually have to disclose if I have a period?' I asked, when prompted to share this piece of information a few days before the fair.

'We treat cultural and religious beliefs very seriously and we cannot afford to insult anybody,' I heard from the spokesperson of the company. He did not give a rat's arse about insulting Botswana by turning it upside down in search of precious stones, but would go to great lengths to please Orthodox Jewish diamond traders who arrived to buy Botswana's heritage.

Forgive me, I did not mean to shout. I got carried away there.

Alicja was furious. She said it was proof that even in the emancipated Western world I was constructed within the boundaries of my femininity.

'Why do you want to change somebody else's country instead of making a difference in your own?' she said during our telephone conversation.

I lied that I needed more time, that it was too soon to proclaim a firm judgment, pack my bags and return to Poland. She reluctantly agreed.

Before I left Poland I had already decided that I wasn't going back. Lying to my family was easy.

I refused to disclose whether I was menstruating or not. On the day of the event I showed up at work as usual. And yes, in case you are wondering now, I did have my period. My curiosity about what was going to happen was larger than the fear of being sacked. Was I going to burn on the spot, or in hell later? You see, I do not respond well to authority.

I was in a lift with three Orthodox Jewish sightholders, squeezed into the furthest corner. I did not have a pen and paper to help me resist the urge to break the silence with my female, unmarried and menstruating voice.

'Excuse me, gentlemen,' I coughed to get their attention. 'The event takes place on the fourth floor and the refreshments will be served on the fifth. Toilets are located on each floor.' All at once, they shouted in Yiddish, their long curled sidelocks bouncing against their cheeks.

Later that day, I was called into the boss's office.

'I heard you were talking to our clients,' he started, without lifting his head from the pile of documents covering his desk.

'Well yes, I wanted to inform them how to find their way around the building.'

'Did they ask you for your opinion?'

'No, but...'

'Exactly,' he said, lifting his index finger in a gesture of silencing me. 'And weren't you informed about not talking to the clients, and specifically not to the Orthodox Jewish diamond traders?' he asked, shaking his finger at me, which was entirely unnecessary. I was a grown, thirty year-old woman, not a kid at school.

'Yes, I was, sir. But I thought they would like to know where the toilets are,.Wouldn't you?'

This time he looked at me. 'Don't get clever with me. Next time do as instructed.'

There was no next time because a month later I was no longer working for the company, which did not surprise me. I would have fired myself. I did not care because I got what I needed – my first job experience and the contact for the supplier of Swazi gold.

Termination of my contract was quick and painless.

'Do you enjoy working for our company?' asked the Human Resources manager. I did not think he expected an honest answer from me so I said yes.

'It's been five months and your maternity cover has come to an end. I am really sorry to inform you that we decided not to extend the contract with you. We don't feel you fit the image of the company. And as you know, we are in a business where each employee is the face of the company. And recently you have not conducted yourself appropriately. Therefore we have come to the conclusion that it would be best if our ways were to part. I am sure you will understand. Besides your contract was a maternity cover, which as far as I am aware has come to its natural end.'

After my dismissal I went to one of the wine bars on Charterhouse Street and waited for Percy Jantjes. He quickly walked in my direction, and before he sat down next to me said, 'Well done. You ruined everything.'

'Fancy a glass of wine or a goodbye fuck?'

'I vouched for you and this is how you repay me?'

'You're just like them.'

'What?'

'You heard me. You talk behind their back, but you're too scared to jeopardize your position by saying something into their faces. What's the word? Ah yes, a hypocrite.'

'You're drunk. Let's go home.'

As much as I was attracted to the childlike curiosity he displayed every time he explored my body with his tongue, and his tireless playfulness during sex, which made the nights we spent together so unexpectedly entertaining, I said no.

'I'm going back to my home. You can go to yours if you like. There's a third option: you can pick up the bill for this bottle of wine.'

'How can you be so selfish?'

'You're angry because I'm not the poor Eastern European girl who needed saving. And it never crossed your mind that maybe it was never about that.'

'I cannot help you to get your job back.'

I had what I wanted. I did not need his help anymore.

Now, I despise people who have no determination in their lives. I had nothing else to do but to stick to my plan. I refuse to succumb to emotional blackmail and, honestly, if you ask me now, any kind of relationship eventually ends in disaster. You see, with losing my job, relations with Percy Jantjes came to their natural end. Whenever I detect in myself that feeling of attachment to somebody or something, you could say that I deliberately construct situations that will release me from this emotional burden. I do not believe in happy endings. Nothing throws people more off-balance than your own metamorphosis in front of their eyes. Nothing throws me more off-balance than my own metamorphosis. Hatred, conflicts, confusions have become the basis of my existence. It is the only way for me to stay in touch with the way things really are. As you remember, I said that the best thing is to love your family from a distance. Of course in your case I am making an exception. That is not to say that I love you, even if we are related to each other, which I still find hard to believe.

It is hot in this room. Let me open the window before I carry on. Don't you just love the birds singing? You can hardly hear them in central London unless you go to one of the parks. Hampstead Heath is my favourite. Maybe I will take you there one day. Or, even better, Chelsea Flower Show in May.

My mother was not interested in flowers or parks or birds when she came with my father on her first visit to London. After I lost my job in the diamond industry I had some time on my hands and I thought to myself: why not invite my parents? It seemed like an impossible idea at first but the gnawing feeling of curiosity about what my parents would make of my new home won over the rational voice in my head, which cautioned me against this step. I bought business class airline tickets, not with the cattle-class airlines but with Lufthansa. I wanted them to feel comfortable, spoil them with over-attentive stewardesses, flood them with my fake affection.

After they arrived, the London Eye was the only tourist attraction my mother wanted to see, she informed me. I must say she enjoyed the views when we were lifted in a pod to over one hundred and thirty metres, snapping away at the panoramic views of the city. Less so Oxford Street, with its crowds making her visibly uncomfortable, bumping her shoulders against hordes of pedestrians. She was lost. On the Underground she grabbed my hand in fear, saying that I was standing too close to the tracks. It had not taken me long to become immune to the place. My mother said she never thought I would willingly choose to live here. 'It's like living in a gutter,' she said, when she noticed mice running across the Underground tracks. They did not bother me.

Almost every day I took my parents out for lunch, usually to English or Irish pubs. My mother did not like the food, unlike my father who ate whatever he was served. Oh, my mother! Poking her fork suspiciously in a cottage pie, she would make a spectacle of loud sighs and accusatory glances, suggesting I was trying to poison her. There was no point convincing her to try something else. Her mind was set. She proclaimed the food inedible, expecting my father to stop eating as well.

'I quite like it,' my father replied, and took another bite of his sausage.

'You've lost your mind,' my mother said and took the fork out of his hand. 'Where are the Polish shops?' she looked at me.

'You came all this way to eat Polish food?' I said.

'I'm worried about you. You have lost weight. You should eat more healthy food.' She gave me an assessing look and fingered my arm before she touched my cheek and ran her fingers along my jaw line.

Healthy food meant a heap of boiled potatoes sprinkled with dill and a piece of pork with a cabbage salad. Or cabbage leaves stuffed with rice and meat, a dish which took at least two days to prepare. I rarely had enough patience to prepare it in my London house, or any other Polish dish which required effort, time and ingredients that I would have had to travel to the other side of London to buy. What a waste of time!

We left the pub and I took my parents to Polanka, a Polish shop on King Street in west London. Once we got there my mother relaxed. She chatted with every shop assistant as if she had known them for many years. She went around the aisles, placing various jars, packets and tins in the basket, filling it to the brim with food I knew I would never eat.

After their return to Poland my kitchen cupboards were littered with cans of chicken meat pate, spicy tomatoes and rice paste, packets of powdered borsch and chicken broth. And in the freezer, bags of mushroom and meat ravioli, sausages. I felt surrounded by silent witnesses from my past. I do not know when exactly I began to feel threatened by what I continued to find in my fridge long after they were gone. I felt guilty that with every passing day the food was going bad, yet I could not bring myself to touch it.

Back home my mother took out all the pots and tirelessly cooked elaborate meals from morning to night, rejecting any invitations to go sightseeing.

'I've seen enough. Why don't you take your father out?' she suggested.

He happily let me take him around London, escaping my mother's presence. My father and I enjoyed meals in Thai, Italian, Vietnamese or Chinese restaurants while we were out. But he always made sure he finished whatever my mother served after we returned home.

'Why don't you tell her we've eaten?' I asked him.

'Let her cook, if she wants to,' he shrugged.

I envied that he could peacefully sit on the sofa and read while my mother's presence ballooned, filling every room with the smells of sizzling pork sausages with onions, boiled ham, cabbage soup. Even opening the windows did not help. My clothes, the furniture, the carpets, were soaked in my mother's cooking. She maintained her authority by conjuring up a little Poland in my kitchen. And when I tried to curb her cooking enthusiasm, she shot accusing glances. Subject closed. I retracted from the kitchen and slumped on the sofa next to my father, powerless.

Although I appreciated that they had agreed to visit me, I was happy to the point of being ecstatic when my parents were

finally gone and I could be on my own without my mother
trying to feed me every hour or complaining about the dirt on
the windows, toilet bowl, bathtub, carpets, television, tables,
walking around every room and scrutinizing every corner as
if her eyes were naturally equipped with a magnifying glass
which allowed her to notice the smallest speck of dust. And
the spiders! The spiders which came out from the mantelpieces
and braced themselves in the middle of the room, staring at her
silently, while she ran after them clutching rolled newspaper
pages with one thought in her mind – to kill. Whatever I left
around or allowed to live had to be killed, disinfected, flushed
or thrown away. She sanitised my house, and my life, against
anything she considered foreign.

Cleaning and cooking was my mother's obsession, setting
me an example of the desirable housewife I should have
aspired to become. She never let me forget where I came from
or what my destiny was. I felt threatened by her ferocious
devotion to housework. At the same time, her organisational
skills astonished me. I must admit the rooms looked almost
immaculate after her visit. Sometimes I even found myself
longing for her devotion to structuring my reality around her
but I quickly choked down this feeling – was it admiration? –
because it was her way of bringing me back to her world, and
going back was never an option for me.

My mother was well informed about the Polish Centre,
POSK, near Hammersmith. I think it was around two days
before they arrived that I received a strange phone call.

'Is your mother there?' a woman's voice asked in Polish.

'Who is this?'

'We will be waiting for Mrs and Mr Rodziewicz in
Lowiczanka. On Saturday. She said she was arriving in London
on Thursday.'

'Who exactly will be waiting?'

'She will know. God bless you.'

On Saturday we took the Circle Line and arrived at Ravenscourt Park tube station and walked towards the POSK building. That was where my mother felt most comfortable in London, among the Poles.

'Courage,' my father whispered while we climbed the stairs, my mother leading and already opening the front door.

Inside, women I did not know surrounded my mother like hens, three hands helping her with her coat, the fourth one releasing my mother's neck from a scarf I had given her as a present.

'My husband and my daughter,' she said, finally remembering we were there, standing at a safe distance.

The women rushed in my direction.

'How old are you?'

'Not married yet? Don't worry, we will find you a boy!'

'Spitting image of her mother.'

Am I? I thought in fear, trying to release myself from their breathing mouths.

We all walked upstairs to the restaurant, Lowiczanka. We were welcomed by waiters with a look of boredom permanently plastered to their tired faces and more Polish food on the menu. I gulped down the first two glasses of wine as if my life depended on it.

The next few hours my mother spent conversing with the women and men who sat at our table, talking about how difficult life must be for them away from the motherland, when they were planning to go back, what the priest was like in their church, whether their grandchildren learned Polish. Before I knew it my mother was introducing me to a young man sitting at the other side of the table.

She squeezed my hand and whispered, 'He comes from a respectable family. Go and talk to him. Is that a third glass of wine you are having?'

'I didn't realise you were counting,' I said.

'He's been watching you since we came in.'

'I'm going for a cigarette.'

But what she meant was that the young man was a white Catholic and probably worked as a lawyer or a doctor or an architect. I hated when she did that, throwing me into the arms of a male victim of her plotting. My aversion to some Polish men I came across, with their condescending egos, as if I was supposed to be grateful they expressed interest in me, only grew stronger. It did not amount to mere annoyance with their presence, but it steadily escalated. Perhaps that was the reason my forced conversations with the prospective marriage candidates never quite resulted in follow-ups.

I took my third glass of wine and walked out on the terrace.

'Hi, I'm Wladyslaw,' I heard a voice behind me.

Why did the men my mother sent to me always have those old fashioned Polish names? Oh, I forgot, because they came from respectable families where naming boys after one of the Polish kings made them somewhat special, like Mieszko or Boleslaw or August.

'Is there something I can help you with?'

'I thought I would introduce myself,' he said. 'I saw you standing on your own.'

'And?'

'You looked kind of sad and lonely.'

'I was thinking.'

'What do you do?' he asked.

'At the moment, I am trying to please my mother.'

'Oh.'

'Sorry, what was your name again?'

'Wladyslaw.'

'Right. Listen, you seem like a nice guy but it was my mother's idea so let's cut the crap. Why don't you find yourself a cute blondie with big Bambi eyes and charm her instead of me? My mother always does it. She introduces me, hoping I'll fall in love with a nice Polish guy and come back to Poland with him. So maybe you should just go, Kazimierzu.'

'It's Wladyslaw.'

'Whatever.'

'You're feisty, you know that?'

I did not like his prolonged laughter and waited patiently until he ran out of air in his lungs.

'Maybe I wasn't clear because you don't seem to be, how can I put this, getting the picture here. I'm not interested in you. I'm simply not interested in getting to know you.' I flipped a cigarette butt on the street below.

'You don't have to be so unpleasant.'

'Do you actually believe I care what you think?'

He shook his head.

'Good. You are not so stupid after all,' I said.

Perhaps I was missing out, letting go of my Prince Charming. But I never stopped to wonder about the possibility of a different life, a 'what if' scenario. In my life there is no place for extra luggage, responsibility for somebody else, their needs, sickness, happiness.

I must admit I became very efficient at getting rid of the potential cavaliers. I mastered the conversations so that I could waste as little energy as possible on getting them out of my face. Which did not please my mother who simply thought I was impolite. 'That's not the way I brought you up,' she would say when we were back home. It did not help when I tried to explain to her that I did not need her to act as a pander because I was perfectly capable of finding a man on my own. At times like that, occasional sex was a perfect antidote.

'I want you to date a nice Polish man who will take care of you. And they go to church, and these people here,' my mother meant the English, 'they don't have God in their lives, and you need somebody who's a good person.'

As if being nice and religious ensures a happy ever after. Besides, I did not leave Poland to end up imprisoned with a Polish husband, preferably a Catholic, with me staying at home, cooking and breeding in a frenzy to please my mother with grandchildren, preferably boys. I am sick of Polish men. I will tell you now that I enjoy my on-and-off relationships in England or Poland, and the men I sleep with are as far as possible from the ideal husband material my mother conjures up in her mind.

If my mother enjoyed trying to find prospective husbands, I did not. Worst of all, she grew even more determined to prove I was wrong, that the only thing I needed was to be exposed to Polish people and culture, and I would open my eyes and accept the gift of motherly judgment.

Once, I think it was during their second or third visit to London, we were just about to leave my place to go to the Polish Centre, POSK. But this time something wasn't right.

'Wear something nicer,' she said. I was standing in the bathroom facing her with her hair in curlers. I was wearing a pair of jeans and a T-shirt.

While I rummaged though my wardrobe in search of an appropriate dress that would please my mother and give me a moment of peace, she meticulously applied make-up in the bathroom. She refused to give me any information. She said it was a surprise. I do not like her surprises. I suspected it was going to be another Polish event, to awaken my Polish soul and a longing for my homeland. Thank God she did not throw photos of Lech Walesa, Pope John Paul II and Frederic Chopin at me.

When we entered the Lowiczanka restaurant it became clear it was a Polish wedding she wanted me to attend. It was a plot she had carefully devised in advance with the librarians from POSK, who had informed her about this celebration.

The continuation of the Polish nation was in full swing. The DJ, dressed in a black shirt and black trousers with a substantial silver chain around his neck and a thin ponytail, was mixing the latest 'Disco Polo' songs. When we came in, he was half way through one of the biggest hits of the evening, Maja, the Bee. Let me give you a brief outline of this popular wedding song. It tells the story of a female bee, Maja, who encounters a male bee, Gucio, while flying from one flower to another, and now Gucio is licking Maja. In the meantime, a group of ants decide to fuck Maja in her arse. The lyrics do not shy away from the details. You could say it was a typical Polish wedding where the more vulgar and coarse the lyrics, unsurprisingly towards women, the more merriment there is among the guests, especially men.

We walked in just as the ants devised the devilish plan to get hold of Maja.

There was a bottle of vodka on each table and I breathed a sigh of relief. My mother waved to a woman sitting at the far corner and we walked across the room to sit down with them. She grabbed my hand and pulled me across the room. My father followed behind us, apologising under his breath for knocking a few tables on his way and causing the guests to grab their glasses to prevent the liquid spilling on the table.

We sat down and a waiter placed three shots of vodka in front of us.

'Cheers to the married couple!' A drunken uncle stood up and raised a glass.

Not drinking vodka at a Polish wedding is not an option. But you still have time to discover its taste so I would not worry about it now.

'Gorzko, gorzko,' everybody was chanting, which is a traditional call for the newlyweds to stand up and kiss in front of the guests. They kiss every time somebody shouts gorzko. As with the vodka, not kissing is not an option at a Polish wedding.

The bride hardly smiled. She was visibly pregnant; although her wedding dress was loose and flowing. you could still see her belly protruding through the material. I looked around.

Most of the guests were at different stages of drunkenness and had eaten a few dishes, judging from the various bowls left unfinished on the tables. Piles and piles of vegetable salads drowning in mayonnaise, cut meats, slices of white bread left half eaten on the side, plates smeared with beetroot with horseradish, hard-boiled egg in mayonnaise. And gherkins, jars and jars of gherkins.

'You should have told me we were coming to a wedding,' I said to my mother.

'I thought you should have some fun,' she said, swaying to the rhythm in her chair.

'And this music, Christ, Mother, what were you thinking?'

'Stop being so grumpy,' she cut me short. 'When was the last time you went to a Polish wedding in London?'

'This isn't my idea of fun.' I wanted to leave. I still had my trench coat on.

'I think it can be a good way for you to get to know new people.' She meant men.

'Great,' I said and poured myself a double shot of vodka.

A few moments later, Wodzirej, a man whose job it is to entertain everybody during the weddings, took a microphone and laid out the rules for the first game. Polish weddings are all about games. I do hope that if you choose to marry one day, although I advise you against it, you will at least think twice before exposing guests to games in the Polish fashion.

Two waiters lined up five chairs in the middle of the room. The bride and four other women chosen by Wodzirej (I was glad he did not pick me) sat on the chairs and lifted their dresses to expose bare knees. The groom had his eyes blindfolded and was now directed to kneel in front of each woman. His job was to touch each knee and guess which one belonged to his newly wedded wife.

'Rub it, rub it,' Wodzirej said. 'It's like in the bedroom, not that you rub her knees but something else.'

The guests burst out in contagious laughter. Finally, the groom raised his hand to indicate he had made his choice. One of the men standing behind him lifted the blindfold. The groom was kneeling in front of the bride who was now folding the material over her knees.

'She taught you well,' Wodzirej shouted. 'Cheers to the married couple!' A forest of hands with shots of vodka flooded the room. 'And now the game with an egg.'

Oh dear, I thought to myself, and hid behind my mother's back.

Wodzirej asked for five couples to come to the dance floor.

'Go and have some fun,' my mother nudged me.

'I don't want to,' I hissed. 'Why don't you go? It seems like you're enjoying yourself.'

'Don't be such a bore.'

'I don't feel like making a fool out of myself.'

My father tried to come to my rescue, 'Elzbieta, leave her alone. If she doesn't want to go, then let her be.' My mother ignored him and waved towards Wodzirej.

'It seems like there's somebody who is a bit shy!' he shouted to the microphone and winked at me. 'Let's give her encouragement.' He started to clap his hands and the rest of the guests joined him.

'Such a lovely lady without a man,' he said and walked to our table. He grabbed my hand and started to pull me from my chair. 'Are there any men here to show this young lady what a real man is like?'

Some young men eagerly shot up from their chairs.

'Fuck off,' I said.

'Magda!' my mother placed her hands on her chest to calm down her racing heart. 'What kind of language is that?'

'You're a wild kitten, aren't you?' he laughed.

'I said fuck off. And get your hands off me. I'm not going anywhere.'

'Don't you want to play with us?' he asked me.

'Does it look like I want to play with you?'

'You don't know what you're missing.'

'I do actually. Now, can you find yourself another victim?'

He walked away to another table where an eager twenty year-old woman was dabbing her cheeks with blusher and displaying her best smile in his direction.

'The gentleman was trying to be nice to you. There was no need to speak to him in such bad language,' my mother said.

'And you dragging me here without even telling me that we're going to a Polish wedding was perfectly fine? Besides, he's not a gentleman.'

'I wanted you to meet new people.'

'I can take care of myself.'

'I can see that.' She shifted in her chair and directed her attention to the guests participating in the next game.

Six couples were now standing on the dance floor and every woman held an egg in her hand. The DJ played the first song. Each woman knelt in front of the man, gently holding an egg against the underside of his leg. Whoever moved the egg up the leg the quickest, without breaking the egg, won. Looking at them I wondered whether the men had brought spare trousers in case there was an unexpected surprise on the way up.

'Ladies, ladies, ladies!' Wodzirej shouted into the microphone. 'Looks like you are very careful with those eggs! Very good. You all have the right touch to handle precious goods!'

'Can we go now?' I asked.

'One more game,' my mother answered.

The waiters placed more bottles of vodka on the tables and more food. I decided to go out for a cigarette. I did not want to smoke inside and I wanted to be alone. Smoking is us Poles' national sport and the small terrace outside the restaurant was already packed with young people standing in clouds of smoke, with their children running around.

There was a woman, in her early twenties, I thought, but it was hard to tell her age because her face was covered in heavy make-up, with tattoos on her bare arms and back – a Polish version of Angelina Jolie. I looked closer. The tattoos were surprisingly similar. Next to her stood a rather bulky man with a bald head. His biceps were about to burst through the sleeves of his jacket. The cloth on his back wrinkled. He stood with his legs wide apart.

'What the hell was it? Huh? Tell me! What was it?' he kept asking, his nose and cheeks reddened by alcohol.

'Oh, stop being so jealous,' she said, exhaling the cigarette smoke.

'Was it fun pushing that egg up that twat's trouser leg? Did you touch his bollocks?'

'Baby, you are overreacting.'

'Am I?' He walked closer to her. 'Am I really? Because it looked to me like you were having lots of fun.' He poked his finger in her chest.

'It's a wedding. Calm down.' She seemed not at all bothered by his outburst. A small boy ran in her direction. 'Come to Mummy, sweetheart.' She lifted the child and gave him a loud kiss, leaving a trace of her lipstick on his chubby cheek. The boy was wearing a white shirt and black trousers. His golden chain hanging from his small neck was the exact replica of his father's.

'I don't want you to take part in any other games. You hear me!' He grabbed her arm.

'Stop shouting at me. And let go of me. You're scaring the boy.' She looked at him with anger. 'Maybe you should stick to beer instead of vodka from now on.' He walked off the terrace. Still holding the boy in her arms, she lit another cigarette.

'Are you okay?' I asked, not that it was my place to get involved with a domestic dispute. I learnt in London that it is best to keep your distance.

'He's always like that after a few drinks. And he's very jealous. We almost didn't come to the wedding. He has got it into his head that I am going to cheat on him. As if he could stop me, even if I wanted to,' she laughed loudly, daring him to come back. 'He can be so dumb.' She put the boy down who ran off after his father.

'Do you?' I asked.

'Do I what?'

'Do you cheat on him?'

'I'm not suicidal,' she laughed, showing off her bleached teeth.

'He looked...'

'Aggressive?' she finished my sentence. 'He's always like that after a few drinks. He's a good man though. He takes good care of me and our son.'

'What does he do?'

'This and that. He's got a construction and transport company. I stay at home most of the time and take care of the family. Are you from the bride or groom's side?'

'Neither. My mother found out about this party and she wanted me to come to meet some guys.'

'I can introduce you to some if you want me to,' she said with a grin.

'No thank you. We're going shortly anyway.' I finished my cigarette.

While I was outside, the next game had begun. The blindfolded groom held a thread in his mouth with a pen attached to the end. An empty bottle was placed in front of him on the floor. The bride was directing him to place the pen into the neck of the bottle. It took them a while to finish the game and when they did, Wodzirej said, 'And this is what the wedding night will look like!'

These demented wedding games were bound to continue until the early morning of the next day, and as it got closer to midnight the level of vulgarity would grow, accompanied by repulsive songs. With a drunken fever descending on all the guests, who slowly became immune to visual and audible stimulus, the atmosphere was growing tawdry. I threatened my mother that the tube would soon close down which, thankfully, was enough to make her leave. My father, too, felt saturated with dubious celebration of wedding happiness.

Of course, just because I do not see the point in exposing my ears and eyes to traditional wedding gaiety (Polish style), it does not mean that others consider this gathering a waste of time. Certainly my mother enjoyed herself, along with the majority of the guests. I did not achieve a renewed appreciation for my countrymen; instead my heart was hardened with increased aversion, especially towards Poles in London.

two

IT WAS DARK and it was raining and I was late for my interview for my second job. I was walking towards the train platform, struggling to open my umbrella. Water hammered from the sky. By the time I managed to cover my head, a bucket of raindrops had found their way behind the collar of my trench coat. It was April, a month after my parents' visit. April, a month when in Poland the sun descends and awakens pedestrians from their winter hibernation. I racked my brain in search of an excuse why I was going to be late. Commuting to central London usually took me twenty minutes on the train, arriving in to Charing Cross. But there was the rain and, as usual, delays were expected.

In front of the stairs leading to the train platform, there was a big pool of water. A while back, I had witnessed the builders sweating as they tried to lay the concrete. They did it at an angle which resulted in directing the rain water towards the bottom of the stairs, rather than away from them.

And so, each time it rained, this highly imaginative decision caused trouble to the passengers, who had no other option but to jump with one foot into the pool in order to get through and climb the stairs towards the platform. Thankfully, there was a second option – clinging to the fence and making your way by placing your feet between each bar. Albeit, slowly!

The people behind the CCTV cameras, installed everywhere 'for your safety and protection,' as you are dutifully informed while waiting for a delayed train, must have been either blind or immune to the ordeal that was happening at the entrance to the platform. Or maybe the cameras never actually worked, which would not surprise me.

The UK rail companies could have saved Londoners this misery by employing proper builders, if making sure the concrete was laid at the right angle turned out to be such a challenging task to them. But what could you expect?

For many in the UK, education stopped being a priority a long time ago.

After I finally fought my way across the fence, balancing an umbrella and a handbag in one hand and clinging to the fence with the other, I felt a compulsion as a citizen, taxpayer and passenger, to make sure the railway staff visualised my morning ordeal.

Here's something you should know about this society before you decide to live here with me: the English can be pussies. Nobody complains about anything. And if you do, you can be certain that nothing will be done. Absolutely nothing!

The ticket officer, the unfortunate recipient of my unrelenting oration, did not flinch for a moment.

'We'll send somebody with a broom,' he said.

The old fashioned broom and a bucket. What a brilliant idea!

But his face said to me: 'I only work here. It's not my fault.'

You see, that ticket officer had a familiar expression I had observed before in London, the look of those who are too unconcerned to do anything, because it is not part of their job description.

'Why do you even bother?' I heard from a fellow passenger behind me who overheard my conversation. 'Every year is the same. Darling, you're wasting your breath.'

I have no religious agenda, no desire to blow anybody up in the name of God, but public services in this country, don't get me started.

Most people are too ignorant to visualise a potential threat in somebody like me, an ordinary citizen, an immigrant, who could become equally, if not more, unstable in pursuit of justice, however you define it. At least the fundamentalist terrorists believe in an ideology with unflinching devotion, pledging their lives to an idea, a dream. And you have to admit; at least they stick to it. I, on the contrary, am a peaceful law-abiding citizen. (Perhaps not all the time as you now know but in the overall picture.) I don't steal, I don't blow up people on the planes and buses, I don't sell drugs to kids on the street. I simply want public transport to work, health professionals to care, banks to stop charging me excruciating service fees I could hardly make sense of, energy companies to get their billing right. Is it too much to ask?

Yes, in those early months in England, I more often began to find myself at a juncture where I – or I should say 'she' because her bloodthirsty desires at times disgust me – yearned for a gun to shoot people; mostly civil servants, sales callers, politicians and bosses of energy companies. And since, as she confidently suspected, she was not the only one with such terminal yearnings, she hoped she could promptly find brothers and sisters in arms in her perfect clean-up programme.

You would think that people who live on an island have had more than enough time, through the centuries, to learn how to deal with the constantly challenging weather conditions, at least the most common ones such as rain and snow. Far from it.

Can I just say that I am telling you all this so that you have a full picture of this place? It's my new home. Despite everything, my cannabis business was welcomed with open hands and warm hearts. I give them that.

You would not remember this, but in 1978 the temperature fell to minus thirty degrees Celsius during the day in some remote parts of Poland. Soldiers and heavy army machinery were used to aid public transport services. The train tracks cracked, buses slowly wheeled in snow tunnels but people still went to work. My mother dressed Alicja and me in thick flannel long johns, trousers, two pairs of orange woollen socks she had knitted herself the previous winter, two pullovers, a woollen scarf, cap and mittens, and with the two of us looking like massive onions of clothes, sent us on our way to school in the mornings. But not in the UK, where the adverse weather conditions – which usually means the temperature falling just below zero – cause the whole country to come to a standstill.

The first time I experienced the threat of snow in London, it was ready to melt in the next few hours and the temperature dropped to a staggering minus two. I did not make it to work because the trains did not come, or was it that the train drivers decided not to go to work? Even some of the tube services had to be suspended because of the snow. While sitting stranded at home, I imagined mice and rats with their mouths open, sticking their tongues out to catch thick snowflakes in the underground in the heat of the tunnels.

The main roads were in total chaos because nobody bothered to grit them. People were unable to walk on the pavements without falling down and subsequently breaking legs because, surprise, surprise, nobody bothered to grit the pavements either. Surely in London – after all it is the capital city – gritting should reach at least some minimal proportions. Nothing could be more misleading. Don't get your hopes up when it comes to public services in London. And whose responsibility is it anyway? After all we all pay every possible tax on the planet for the privilege to live in this First World capital. Well, strictly speaking I do not but many do.

In the midst of all this the BBC, which prides itself on its professionalism and astute journalism, devoted more time to the polar bears having fun in the snow in London Zoo or people building snowmen outside their houses than proper criticism of the local councils and services which fail year after year to remove snow on time. And it never occurs to anybody to sack the bastards responsible for the public transport disorder! But that requires accepting Outlook invitations to more than one meeting, PowerPoint presentations, Excel sheets with cost calculations, video conferencing with India to outsource the services to save the costs and numerous email exchanges, before it reaches a bullet-point action plan, which then needs to be printed, bound and distributed to all interested parties.

Now, feeding her ulcer with a boiling anger of a fight nobody cared about, I made my way to the platform in the rain. I am telling you now that if you decide to come with me to London, save yourself the trouble and embrace the commuting experience. Save yourself high blood pressure, a stroke or a heart attack, and go with the flow. Be wiser than I was. There are very few things I miss from Poland, but public services are something I envy people who live there.

'It's late again,' I said to a fellow passenger standing right next to me.

'Yes.'

'I wonder if it will come at all.'

'Probably not.'

We stood in silence, looking into the horizon and hoping for a train to come. Like two lonely cowboys waiting to hear the noise of the train engine, except that there were at least forty of us on the platform hoping for exactly the same thing.

'Why did you say probably not? They're showing that it's running late. There's still a chance the train may arrive,' I said.

'Well, you know,' he said, 'I have this theory; I was jotting down times for the Arsenal – Chelsea London derby. And every time there is one, the train is either late or never comes. I have formulated this theory that the train driver is too pissed to come to work.' He vigorously shook the rain water from his collar.

I kept my ramblings about the misgivings of the public services to myself but I was pleased I had found a fellow soul in this maddening place. It helped me to regain some flimsy idea of hope in humanity, at the time when I was about to obliterate any form of stupidity in my vicinity.

When the next train arrived, we fought our way in. Of course, it was almost impossible to squeeze inside. With mental and physical perseverance commuters on London trains during rush hour guard their spots as if their life depends on it. Pleading, shouting or threatening rarely works, triggering little reaction among the ones trapped inside. Occasionally, you get a joker who shouts back, 'Do you want to sit on my lap beautiful?' But more often it is simply 'Where?'

This time we managed to push our way in and ended up sardined in the radiating heat of heavily perfumed bodies. But the olfactory experiences are not limited to various floral bouquets, as at this point I found myself whiffing the scent of weed. The man, on whose chest my breasts found a resting place, protested with a weak smile.

To say that the railway industry in the UK has earned a special place in my life is a gross understatement. Not only because of the pool of water which becomes a challenge every time it rains, especially when the pool gets bigger and deeper, dangerously reaching the first bar of the fence and hindering my climbing; the rain and snow which always affect the timetable; but also the most amazing working hours of the railway workers who relentlessly fix the tracks over the weekends.

Perhaps if I tell you about a recurring lucid dream I had been having you would be able to understand me and her better. It is the middle of the night, interrupted by the drilling and pandemonium of noise generated by a rail worker over zealously hitting the nails and bolts. She cleans her AK-47. She whispers to it and rubs it gently, then she assembles the grenades on the kitchen table. She opens the back door to the garden and starts shooting everything that moves. Just to be on the safe side, she uses RPG-7 as a final goodbye to the noise. She goes back to her bedroom and falls asleep like a baby.

Why are you crying? Did she scare you? Please, oh please, don't be afraid of her. Look, I am smiling, there's nothing you should fear in me. Now, let's wipe those tears off your pretty face. It's only my hand, there's no need to move your face away. I promise I never killed anybody. Not personally, at least. What did I say? Oh, nothing, just talking to myself. You must admit though it is exhilarating to be able to do what you want, without fearing the consequences. Dreaming your own reality begins the process of creating your own destiny. It did for me. And yet … your eyes are welling up with tears again. I will stop, for I think your distress over my words is drawing your attention to the part of my dealings you are not ready to hear about in its entirety. I won't mention killing people again. Let me go back to my story, my next cover job.

I did not make it to the interview on time. But nobody did that day. Mind you, it was an interview with a new job agency so I was not bothered about being late.

When the agent finally arrived I was asked a familiar question I heard too often: 'Are you sure you are eligible to work in the UK?'

You see, I was still getting used to being treated with an uncomfortable suspicion about my status. Not many people knew which countries joined the EU in 2004. And after I waved my national insurance card in front of the ignorant agent and flashed my best smile I received an awkward sigh of relief.

After I lied my way through the first set of questions about my job experience in England and in Poland, and sweated over language and computer tests, I was finally sent for an interview for a rolling part-time temporary contract as an assistant in a telecom company. I got the next cover job.

The first few months I was bored to death. No savvy fashionistas to tell me what to wear. No Orthodox Jews. No blood diamonds hidden in the vaults. I did not have much work to do but the money was better than in my previous employment. Not that it mattered with my expansion plans for the weed business. I was making progress. I was steadily Anglicized. I kept my mouth shut and I smiled more often. A development I kept hidden from Alicja, and especially from my mother who would surely label me a traitor.

By now I had already set up two small cannabis gardens, one in a basement where I grew around twenty plants in dirt, and the second in a small greenhouse in the backyard of my house where I began to experiment with aeroponics. I painted the windows with white paint. Although the house I lived in had tall bushes and trees around it, I was very careful. I told my neighbours I was growing indoor tomatoes, and I did. The tomato garden occupied a small part of the greenhouse. In the other section I set up two sealed tubes with five cannabis cuttings in each tube. I experimented with nutrient teas, animal-based fertilizers, various liquid organic multivitamins, and watched the buds grow. I was amazed. The growth rate was double compared to a soil system. I needed a bigger – a much bigger – space.

I needed a shipping container.

While I meticulously planned the next step in my cannabis production, I almost began to worry that my work life in London would remain uneventful.

One day I was sitting on a bench outside the office building, smoking a thin menthol cigarette, when an English contractor for the same company joined me.

'Do you mind if I sit next to you?'

'Not at all, please.' I moved to make space for him. He took a cigarette from a packet of Marlboro Lights and I handed him my lighter.

'Magda Rodziewicz.'

'Patrick Webb, Head of Research,' he said with a polite smile. Then he asked me if I was Polish and said that he heard a lot about me in the company. 'I love Polish people. I worked in Poland on various contracts a few years back, in Warsaw.'

In fairness, Patrick was the first person I had met in London who actually knew where Poland was located on the map and had an impressive knowledge of our culture and customs. I must admit that the few sentences he then said in Polish made an impact on me, considering how difficult and daunting our language seems to everybody. Seven cases for nouns, adjectives and pronouns; a complex gender system; verbs inflected according to gender, person and number; variable word order in one sentence; not mentioning elaborate orthography with a number of diacritics, and the pronunciation, is more than enough to put off anybody from learning such an complex system of communication. I don't want to discourage you but you are facing that as well.

At the end of our cigarette break he offered me a place on his team. Patrick did not need to convince me. I was ready to welcome any change to bring some drama to my boring office life. It was liberating.

The months were passing slowly and I would not be lying if I said that I settled in. But sometimes Patrick would put me in awkward situations.

'There're seven of you in the room and you can't come up with anything remotely resembling a solution. Magda is far more intelligent than all of you.' Such outbursts invited looks of jealousy especially from other assistants but made Alicja proud of my steady development, which I reported in regular phone calls to her.

'Finally somebody has recognised your talent,' she said.

'I think my talents lie somewhere else,' I responded, looking out through the window at the greenhouse.

Soon I found a new friend in the office.

Lorraine was an accounts manager. Every Friday after work we would go out for drinks to one of the wine bars in Covent Garden. The office was a five-minute walk from the market.

'I'm in love,' Lorraine announced one evening.

'Great,' I responded with less excitement in my voice. 'Who's this mystery man? You never have time for me these days?'

She could not stop herself from beaming. 'He works in the same building with us. His name is Neville Hunt,' she said.

'How long have you been seeing each other?'

'Two months. I know it's not long but, Magda, he's the one.'

'Meaning what exactly? You want to get married or something?'

She vigorously nodded her head while biting her lower lip. A few streaks of her hair got caught in one of her round earrings.

I almost choked on my gin and tonic. 'But you barely know each other,' I said. I looked for a tissue in my handbag to wipe the wet patches from the drink I had spilt on my shirt.

'I know,' she said, 'but there is such chemistry between us.'

'You need to slow down a bit. I really want you to be happy but you can't jump at a guy without getting to know him first. You know what I'm talking about; socks on the floor, dishwashing, bills to pay. In case you missed the picture, it's called real life.'

I could almost hear Alicja's voice ringing in my ears, saying how ironic it was for me to utter such wise comments, especially as I am so openly against getting married. I do not believe in marriage. I do not think I am emotionally normal. What do you think? Oh, forget it.

'I know, I know,' she said. I was getting a strange feeling it was going to end badly.

'Let me be happy.' Lorraine placed her hand on mine to reassure me that she knew what she was doing and that I was simply a sceptic.

'All right, girl, just keep your eyes open,' I said. I resigned myself to witnessing what she was going to do next.

But you see I am a sceptic. Even when Alicja told me she was getting married to Krzysiek, shortly after their graduation from the university, I had doubts about him. Stories about Krzysiek's promiscuous past, the boozy nights with female students, were not enough for Alicja to rethink her decision. I almost wanted to take her and meet all the women his friends claimed he had been with and ask her if she had any idea who he really was? How do you know who the person you think you love actually is? How do you know which part of you is the real self, the real you, and which part is an image you skilfully conjure in front of the others?

Krzysiek always made a good impression with my mother, maybe because he reminded her of my docile father, and that was enough for my sister, to get the seal of mother's approval. After all who knows what is best for you if not your parent? And Krzysiek never questioned my mother's authority. Neither did my father. My sister settled on whatever he told her about himself. He can be quite convincing as you will find out later. Alicja wanted to believe in Krzysiek's innocence, because he was a rock to build a castle on, as she had told me a few weeks before their wedding. I wanted her to believe it too, perhaps more than she did, because Krzysiek and I, we ... let me stop here. I will tell you more tomorrow. For now let's focus on me and Lorraine.

The romance began to evolve so I saw even less of her. I do not understand what throws women like Lorraine into complete oblivion once they fall in love. As if she was afraid to spend time with me because that would mean she was not sufficiently devoted to Neville. It did not stop him from seeing his friends; I often noticed him leaving the office with other men and going to the pub opposite the office. Lorraine's behaviour was psychologically interesting to me. She wanted to be loved. It was almost as if she was condemned to wanting to be loved and if she did not devote her entire time to the object of her feelings it would mean betrayal. You see, the women of my generation, at the age of thirty and above, reach a point where they can't allow themselves to wait endlessly because with every passing year their chances to sweep up a man with their long-gone innocence are simply nonexistent. At the age of thirty you have pretty much developed your habits to the point where you are not going to do anything about them. You come as a package. You either take it or leave it. I always thought that men occupied a rather privileged position in our society when it comes to relationships, simply because it is easier for them to have a younger partner. For women it is not so simple, or socially acceptable. Lorraine was one of those women, blinded by their biological clock and the desperation that comes with passing time.

Soon afterwards Lorraine told me that Neville was already married.

'He doesn't love his wife. He said he'll divorce her,' she said.

'Dump the guy,' I told her.

'You don't understand what real love is about. It's not what you think. He's going to propose to me. You better start looking for a dress. I'd like you to be a bridesmaid.'

'Is he going to divorce his wife before or after he gets married to you?' I asked.

But she was already thinking about a Pronovias wedding dress. In the end, it was her life, not mine. Who was I to lecture her on faithfulness? I certainly should be the last person to advise Lorraine. My past, like my present, was complicated.

In the middle of my second black coffee Lorraine sent me an email requesting an urgent meeting outside the building. It was almost seven months since their relationship began. I thought it was one of those he-loves-me-so-much moments and did not think much of it. I did not respond at once. She phoned me a few minutes later.

'Haven't you got my email?' I heard her shaky voice. Was she crying at her desk?

'I have but I'm busy. Sorry, honey, what's up?'

'Meet me outside.'

I took a pack of cigarettes from my desk and went to the lifts.

I saw her standing at the far end of the courtyard, close to the fence. I could tell she was crying. And because I had not seen her for two months, I had not realised how much weight she had lost. It was then it dawned on me what a toll this relationship had taken on Lorraine.

'What happened?' Now I really began to worry about her, seeing her so physically fragile and mentally destroyed.

'I know you told me, but please, please, just listen to me.'

'All right. Calm down. What's going on?'

'Neville dumped me. Remember when I told you he had a wife? Well, that's not everything. She is seven months pregnant.' She finished quietly without looking at me.

The children. They usually arrive at the least expected moments in life.

'Let me get this straight. He said he has a wife and wants to get married to you, but forgot to mention this tiny detail that his wife's been pregnant all this time?' I did not mean to shout at her but my anger at her gullibility and stupidity made me lose control.

I had to light a cigarette for her as she struggled to make the lighter work with her fingers trembling. 'I know you told me to dump the guy and wait until he gets a divorce, but please don't tell me "I told you so". I can't take it anymore.'

'Too late now.'

'Last weekend I decided to confront him. I went to his house to tell his wife that we were in love and that he was planning to divorce her. Neville's wife opened the door. You can imagine how I felt, when I suddenly found myself standing face to face with her, and her belly,' she cried.

'Yes, I think I get the picture,' I muttered shaking my head. 'But going to his house?'

'I was desperate!' she shouted, but quickly composed herself and carried on, 'Neville rushed his wife inside the house and stood outside with me talking. He said that he was sorry, and it was over and to leave him alone or he'd call the police. He actually said it was over. To my face.'

I was not sure who I was more upset with: her, for such stupidity blinded by passionate emotion; or him, for being such a dick, who simply had to have a girl to shag for seven months, while his wife was preparing to give birth to their first child.

Lorraine made me promise I would not try to talk to him. I agreed reluctantly.

Three weeks later Lorraine and I met in a wine bar after work. She was laughing nervously and wanted to show me something. She waited until the waitress opened a bottle of wine and placed it on our table before she explained what it was about.

'Listen, do you remember the security guy we sometimes hang out with?' she asked, anxiously looking over my shoulder towards the window.

'Jerome.'

'He printed an email Neville sent to his line manager. By the way, I think he likes you.' She smiled coyly.

'Yes, well, he and I are kind of having sex together.'

'Kind of?'

'What was the email about?'

'Here.' She placed three pages of A4 in front of me. 'Read it and tell me what you think.'

Sweet Jerome. I knew I could count on him to keep an eye on Lorraine when I was not around. When he happily offered me a spliff with Jamaican Sensi after our first lovemaking I knew there was the potential for us to do business together. You see, Jamaican Sensi was a type of cannabis I had not yet had the pleasure of smoking, so I welcomed Jerome's offer.

I moved my wine glass and read with interest.

On 14 August Lorraine Williams lured me into a meeting room on the ground floor after working hours. She locked the door and pushed me against the chair. She kneeled in front of me and unzipped my trousers. Then she ordered me to have sexual intercourse with her. I responded: 'No, Lorraine. I am a married man.' But she would not stop. It was not the first time when she forced me to have sex with her despite the fact I am happily married and my wife is expecting a baby. I thought that this behaviour would finish but she is uncontrollable.

Not a word about the seven-month affair. After I finished reading I thought Neville should consider a career change and become a writer of popular novels saturated with sex scenes. Yet, the consequences of his rape accusation were serious enough to stop me from laughing at what I had just read.

'Why are you getting yourself involved in this?' Alicja asked, when I left outside to call her and seek her advice, even if she was not familiar with the British legal system. Still, she was a lawyer, a corporate lawyer, but nevertheless.

'How can I not get myself involved? Lorraine's my friend.'

'You're going to lose your job. It's not worth it.'

My sister was jealous because I had finally found somebody she thought I cared about. Suddenly the loyalty I showed towards my new English friends was a threat, because it made her believe I was forming a bond with somebody other than my sister. But nobody could replace Alicja in my life. How could she not see that? You see, my parents were one thing I was certain about leaving behind, but leaving my twin sister was something else. We are, we were, inseparable. Complete loyalty and devotion formed the basis of our sisterly bond. I know what I said earlier about relationships. This one was the most difficult for me to navigate through.

'Besides,' she continued, 'it's none of your business.'

'Are you saying this as a lawyer or as my sister? I would appreciate some understanding here.'

'What does it have to do with anything?'

'Is that what you recommend, professionally I mean, for me to back off?'

'You take things too personally.' Her voice was steady, like when she described the cases she was working on at work. I almost felt I was one of her clients, when she delivered her dry legal speeches to them. I usually admired her intimidating professionalism, but not today.

'I care about Lorraine otherwise I wouldn't be calling you for advice. But, at the same time, she's to blame. She's intoxicated with an image she created in her mind. She made herself believe he was somebody he wasn't. Women endlessly chase the dream of a happily ever after, with a Prince Charming who will whoosh them into the sunset, even if they don't want to admit it. They're capable of fitting anybody into their imaginary box, with a "happy every after" inscription across the lid.'

'Are you saying that Krzysiek is my Prince Charming?' Alicja asked. I detected a quiver in her voice.

'You and Krzysiek both love each other, and he's not married to somebody else. And I guess in a way, yes, he is your Prince Charming. But now I'm talking about women like Lorraine. At the end of the day, women are to blame for being so stupid as to trust and never learn, always making the same mistake, falling in love with a person they subconsciously know is not right, or married. No self-control. But here we are.'

She said somebody entered her office and she had to go. I wondered if I had said too much, if she had deliberately cut this conversation short.

After Patrick patiently listened to the whole story, he was sympathetic and said he would support Lorraine if her case got picked by the Human Resources department. It was down to Neville's line manager to respond to this rape accusation. The irrationality of that email, the disproportionate description of what really took place – I could hardly imagine Lorraine forcing herself on a man like Neville with his one hundred and eighty pound body – became the dramatic development in office life that I seemed to have been waiting for.

A few weeks later I was en route to see one of Patrick's managers when I bumped into Neville on the staircase. He acted as if nothing happened, greeting me with his customary, 'Are you all right, doll?' I was disquieted by his relaxed face with a trace of smirk playing on his lips. A sly smile betrayed him, and I realised, at this moment, there was no going back. His claim to fame was scoring Lorraine and he already knew he got away with it.

I was just about to break the promise I had made to Lorraine and speak to him. I could not help myself. Lorraine was too polite to express what I, what the woman I bury under my smile, never has problems with saying out loud. Call it a female bond, or sisterhood. She had a soft spot for Lorraine.

'What the fuck were you thinking?' she asked.

'Excuse me? I don't understand what you're referring to,' he answered, his eyes dancing on me. He was towering over my five foot two frame.

'Is that so?' she braced herself on the stairs and placed her right arm on the railing, preventing him from passing. 'Are you a real douchebag or just desperately trying to join the club? Because you're on the right track, I can tell you right now.'

'I still don't know what you are talking about.' He remained composed.

'Lorraine. Remember her?' He grimaced. 'What was this relationship about? Was it about your male ego? Was it just a score for you? What the fuck were you thinking? The girl fell in love with you, you idiot! And you simply let her, knowing all this time you would never give her what she wanted. If you can't keep your dick in your pants, don't get married and then shag around like your life depends on it. Have you thought about your wife and child? What kind of person are you?'

'Tough shit.'

'Don't you fucking dare come near her again or make ridiculous rape claims.' That got his attention. The smirk on his face was immediately gone.

'Are you threatening me? How do you know about the rape claim?'

'What does it look like I am doing? Do you need me to spell it out for you?'

'I think you've made yourself clear enough.'

'Maybe your wife hasn't pussy-whipped you enough, but I hope she will, after the birth of your child.'

Not waiting for his response, she opened the door and walked through the corridor towards my desk.

I did not have to wait long for the outcome of her rant. The next week on Monday I had a meeting with the head of Human Resources. I was informed about a complaint made against me for my verbal abuse and threats to one of the members of the company.

'Are you talking about Neville Hunt?' I asked, tired of the "corporate confidentiality" bullshit.

'We are not allowed to disclose the name of the person making a complaint,' said the woman sitting opposite me. Her eyes were firmly set on me, trying to assess how threatening I could be to the company if I pursued legal action.

Human Resources acted like the Holy Inquisition; they had already made up their minds about the outcome of this situation. The royal 'we' informed me about my contract coming to an end, and that they were seriously thinking about not extending it. 'In the light of your gross misconduct, and as we are fully committed to the wellbeing of all our employees,' I was politely informed. The office campaign to terminate my contract had already started.

The truth was, I no longer cared. The corporate hierarchy favoured permanent workers over temps, and getting rid of Neville would cost the company seven years of his faithful service against my weekly rolling contract. You see, it is never about who is right or wrong, who produces better evidence, but the cost to the company. Still, I tried to make the point that the conversation I had with the person filing a complaint, aka Neville Hunt, took place on the staircase and was private, but I was quickly contradicted, 'Technically, you were in the building, thus your misconduct took place on the company's premises.'

The same week, around five on Friday, I was waiting outside the office building with Patrick for some clients, who had invited us for a drink after work. I told him about the conversation I had with Human Resources on Monday.

I noticed a woman from the job agency that had placed me in this company walking towards me. She told me the telecom company had called her and asked her to come, nothing more than that. After a short while Jerome came out and asked me and my agent to go back to the building.

We were welcomed by a young Human Resources manager I had never met before.

'What's it about?' I asked. I was impatient to get it over with.
'You will soon find out.'

The manager walked in front of us trying to open each door on his way. I read somewhere that apparently losing a job generates the same amount of stress as a death in the family. You would think Human Resources should be well acquainted with this data. But Human Resources are not created for the benefit of the employees, rather for the employers, to save them from potential lawsuits. I was slowly learning this new game of office pretence.

'Ah!' the manager exclaimed, proud of himself when he finally pressed the handle and the doors opened. 'Please, come in,' he said. My agent followed first. She and I sat at one end of the room and the man on the other. He took out some documents from his bag and put them on his lap. He sat erect and focused.

'On behalf of the company I would like to inform you that we will no longer require your services. I will need your laptop and mobile phone back. Please return them now. You don't need to show up at work on Monday.' He delivered the message in a dry voice.

'You can't release me from my duties just like that. I need to inform the clients,' I said.

'It has been taken care of,' was the reply.

My agent looked at me but said nothing. This company was their biggest account. If the client said they wanted somebody out, the agency was expected to do whatever the client requested.

'Has my boss been informed about this situation?' I asked.

'Yes, your boss has been informed.'

I could not believe Patrick wouldn't tell me so I carried on, 'Who's my boss?'

The manger fidgeted in his chair, 'As I said, your boss has been informed.'

'I want to hear the name of my boss,' I pressured him.

'As I said, your...'

'I heard you the first time,' I interrupted him. 'I want to hear the name of my boss.'

'Susan Young,' he answered, at last.

'Susan Young isn't my boss but a line manager reporting to my boss, Patrick Webb, whom I'm going to call right now.' I dialled Patrick's number and waited for him to answer his mobile phone, while looking at the man in front of me. I continued, 'I'm very curious what he'll have to say when he finds out about this situation.' I heard Patrick's voice and said, 'Patrick, I've just been sacked. Could you please come to the meeting room number eight on the ground floor?'

The manager fixed his tie and jacket. Patrick used to belong to the Special Boat Service and I had no idea what he was going to do. Sabotage and survival in the thickest jungles of the world, killing drug lords, training American SEALs, were Patrick's daily tasks in his younger days. This Human Resources manager could have been squashed like a bug by Patrick's little finger. Patrick never spoke openly about his past, as the SBS obliged him to sign a confidentiality agreement, but occasionally he would lift the lid to me.

'We were walking in a jungle,' he started in a quiet voice while we sat in a wine bar over two glasses of Singapore Sling.

'Where? Which country?'

'A jungle, Magda. What difference does it make?'

'Sorry.'

'There were seven of us, heavily geared up. Our aim was to eliminate the drug lords who hid in one of the villages. We were walking a path in total silence through thick foliage next to a bog, when suddenly, a huge snake came down from one of the branches above heads and lifted up the first soldier. It was a reticulated python. The guy was gone before our eyes, in a split second. There was nothing we could do.'

If there was anybody who could help me now, it was Patrick. A few moments later he quietly opened the door and walked in. Despite his turbulent past, Patrick was the most peaceful person I had ever encountered.

The manager got up, extended his hand and introduced himself.

Patrick kept standing, 'You're saying that Magda is being released from her duties as of now?'

The manger cleared his throat and said yes.

'I would like you to leave the room,' Patrick said to me.

Impatiently, I was pacing the corridor for about ten minutes before I saw him come out.

'I resigned,' he announced.

'What?'

'I told them I can't work without my right hand. Not only was I not informed about this decision, it's unacceptable. I can't work in such conditions. I told them I am leaving unless they bring you back. I've given them two days to rethink their actions.'

I must say that I was impressed. I never expected such loyalty from somebody I worked with.

He also arranged for me to keep the laptop and the mobile phone until Monday morning when I was supposed to show up at seven to clear my desk.

It was obvious we were not going to join the clients for drinks. Instead, Patrick and I had to discuss a plan of action. In all this, it was good to see that the clients were even more surprised than us, but they got used to not questioning the personnel politics of the companies they were contracting for. People came and went with no explanations provided. Inquisitiveness into the reasons behind such abrupt decisions was not welcomed.

That night Patrick and I tried to call almost every senior person involved in the project. Conveniently, everybody's phone was switched off. Sitting and nodding our heads to a voice of a jazz singer and her band in a wine bar, Octave, we spent a whole night topping up on Singapore Slings and Mai Tais. Under the influence of the drunken cloud and in the spirit of honesty I made phone calls to people who were never fond of me. Neville was one of them. I swore. It was not the greatest moment of my life and I didn't share it with Alicja. Despite Patrick's assurance that he would do everything in his power to reinstate me I didn't think the company would take me back. I admired his willingness to fight for me but it was not worth it.

I awoke in total darkness before dawn the next day. I was mentally exhausted and yet I could not go back to sleep. I tossed in bed, trying to make up my mind what I should do next. I opened the company's laptop and wrote an email to some contractors with a short message about the termination of my contract, and my contact details in case they wanted to get in touch with me. Or in case anybody had an opening and I could apply for a new job. In the midst of the recent events I wanted to preserve self-respect. I refused to subscribe to the code of silence surrounding the circumstances of my dismissal.

On Monday morning I showed up in the office just before seven to return the company's laptop and mobile phone, and pick up my belongings from the office. Shoes, a few books and some photos were all that I left behind. I was escorted to the fourteenth floor by Jerome.

An office circus. What did the company expect I would do? Smash the monitors on my way up? Or maybe go commando-style and shoot my colleagues? I would never do anything to jeopardize my cannabis business. Losing my cover job was not the worst thing that could happen to me. Another reason why you should not form attachments with the people you work with. Lesson number five. All relations in life are temporary. Losing your job is a given. It is only a matter of time but it will happen eventually. Now you understand why having a double life, a double income, is vital in surviving whatever life throws at you.

'Darling, I'm so sorry about all this,' Jerome said, whilst we walked towards the lifts. He wanted to touch me but too many people were already observing us with curiosity.

'Don't worry about it,' I told him with a smile. 'Besides, I've already told the boys to deal with the cunt.'

I fondly remembered how he licked and bit her neck when they ended up in the office toilet for the disabled. It was one of those evenings when after a few drinks I realised I had left my mobile phone on my desk and went back to the building. It was around nine and Jerome walked with me to my floor. But on the way up, in the lift, they were already sucking on each other's tongues and lips, pulling each other's clothes off. Thankfully there was hardly anybody in the office when they stumbled out of the lift, half undressed and searched for a toilet. She pressed on his chest with one hand, forcing him to sit down on the toilet seat, while she lifted her skirt to take off her underwear. He grunted when, with her back to him, she let him in between her thighs. His eyes were closed when she twisted her head to look at his face. She liked looking at his fingers pinching her nipples, releasing them and then clasping her full breasts in his both hands. He held her tight when he came, sinking his teeth into the back of her neck, so tight she ran out of breath. The danger of being caught was seductive. She consistently rejected his offers to spend more time together. She liked the fact they did not have to stay in each other's presence and pretend to have a conversation after sex. That sex led to something deeper. She and I have a fetish on personal space. The last thing she needed was to be forced to explain or curb her habits for the sake of living with somebody else. She and I were far away from imposing personal restrictions which would inevitably come when you lived with someone. She did not consider making the relationship work apart from those sexual encounters they shared and the Jamaican Sensi cuttings he supplied her with.

Jerome waited until I finished packing all my belongings and then he escorted me back to the lifts. The Human Resources manager I had met on Friday joined us and, with severity chiselled into his face, observed my every move, eager for me to leave the building.

It goes without saying that it was my fault the contract was terminated. Nonetheless, I felt I did the right thing when I attacked Neville. The boys did a good job as well. Of course, in the immediate aftermath of my experience I became obsessed with dissecting each day what went wrong. But most importantly, what was wrong with me? I was reminded about my place, where obedience and submission was rewarded. I began to exist in an endless process of dissecting my own identity, of self-evaluation, comparing what I said and did with the people I worked with, trying to find a way to behave and speak like them, to become one of them. Was it really possible? This creation of me was not a likeable person. Even less so now. But then I was still confused. Deep inside she has no intention of becoming a desired member of this society, or any society if I am to be honest. The exaggerated excitement which I felt when I first came to London gave way to something sinister which can be summed up as follows: If you don't want to be screwed, screw first. This, I say, is the crucial motto of today.

'If I had a gun I would go back to the office and kill them all,' I said to Alicja after I informed her about my dismissal. She had called me on Skype. 'Or perhaps just Neville and the people from Human Resources, and job agents for good measure.'

'You aren't supposed to say things like that.'

'Everything's fine as long as you keep your mouth shut and don't confront anybody. If that happens, then it suddenly becomes inappropriate, politically and socially incorrect. There's no middle ground.'

'Still you should stop talking about shooting people.'

'It was a metaphor,' I said, trying to ease her anxiety. 'It gets better. The head of the job agency, after they asked to see me to inform me about possible legal action because I sent an email to the clients over the weekend, told me they did not see any new jobs suitable for me. Of course they didn't. The moment she said that I knew I had become a liability to the agency. The reason why they didn't want to send me for another interview was to save themselves the embarrassment, if I exhibited my disposition not to comply within the corporate environment again. They would not take the risk with me. I was condescending towards authority and she knew it.'

'Unless you're prepared to be flexible,' here she waited for me to reassure her that I was willing to work on my ways but I let her talk instead. '...Well, you know what I mean.'

'I have a meeting with the clients in two weeks. Patrick has already arranged it and they can help me to get a new job.'

'You don't make it easy on people, you know that.'

'It's not my problem,' I said, looking for a lighter underneath the newspapers scattered on the table. I really wanted to confess it was that thing inside me, that monster I gave birth to, my twin with an unwritten contract, which couldn't be erased from my memory.

'Well, it is. If you want to keep a job longer than few months.'

'Being nice doesn't solve the problem,' I said.

'It's almost as if you were taking pleasure in antagonising people. And I know you're not like that.'

'You think you know me that well?'

I gave up on the subject. I was beginning to find it difficult to explain myself. I was not sure whether it was the short telephone conversations or rare emails (Alicja never had the time to write lengthy emails), that prevented me from convincing her. Or was it just a poor excuse? I was changing. I had entered a process of metamorphosis, of eradicating excessive emotionalism. I was becoming the other. Still, I was so confused in those days. Was

I really me? Or was she who spoke with my voice and had my face the true me? If there was somebody who could truly hurt me that was Alicja. Alicja wouldn't hurt her, but it was me, or whatever remained of me. My inclination towards emotional destruction – or should I say experimentation with human nature – took a new turn. If I was to see whether the 'she' inside me could eradicate any form of belonging I would have to go further than extracting myself geographically. I would have to go back to face my family on their own ground. My true adversary was waiting for me in Poland.

I think I will make a black coffee for myself. The whole house is empty so I can safely go to the kitchen without bumping into anybody. You just wait for me. Silly me, where would you go? I will bring an apple juice for you. My mother tells me it's your favourite.

I am definitely addicted to coffee. I didn't realise it was so late. But we still have some time left before I leave you with my mother and go back to the hotel for the night. Oh, you know, it is easier for everybody if I do not stay for too long in this house. The arguments, explanations, justifications, it all tires me these days. The funeral is in five days, so we still have some time before we will have to participate in this circus. Did I mention my mother asked Father Maciej to conduct the ceremony? It seems like he is the best person to do it since he has known our whole family for all these years.

When Patrick arranged the meeting I did not realise it would open an opportunity for me to take my revenge on the people who were responsible for losing my previous employment.

'What can I do?' The client went straight to the point. I liked that.

'Can you get Magda a job?' Patrick asked.

'The head of a project in the Department of Health is looking for an assistant. Part time, though. Would you be interested?'

'Perfect,' I said. 'Is it for Campbell?'

Who didn't know Campbell? He was the most feared person in the telecom company. Campbell was like a raging bull. I saw him a few times in the reception area spitting at the security men who opposed Campbell leaving his bicycle inside the building. He was a healthy type, a non-smoker, and insisted on cycling around central London. Good luck!

'Why not?' I said. 'I didn't know he was recruiting. Considering that for the last seven months I worked on the delivery side, it would make sense as I know what the project is about.'

'Good,' the client said. 'In that case I'll send your details to his office.'

After we finished the meeting and Patrick and I were on our own, he asked, 'Are you sure you want to do this?'

I was touched by his concern. What else could happen? I decided I was going to throw myself into the new opportunity. It was almost a done deal. I did not have to deal with another job agency. Besides, I was curious.

'You know what they say about Campbell,' he continued. 'But somehow I don't think you should have any problems. You're a tough cookie. You can handle it.'

'I can always leave, can't I?' I said. 'Besides, after all the shit I've been through, I think people in the telecom company would be very surprised to see me working on the other side.'

He agreed.

Two weeks after meeting with the client, I had an interview with Campbell. I smiled and nodded, and was soon offered the job. Whether I got the job because of my experience at the telecom company or a client's recommendation, it did not really matter.

Before I began to work with Campbell, I had to undergo a comprehensive security check, which delayed my start date for another few weeks. I kept my anarchist comments, as well as my small cannabis garden at home, hidden. I needed a cover job, not another drama in my life. Luckily, the security services, which were responsible for the checks performed on new employees across various government offices, did not pick up on my views. It felt reassuring to know that Big Brother, watching over society, took its job thoroughly and seriously.

three

I CANNOT HELP BUT FEEL slightly unnerved when I visit Poland. It has become a voyeuristic experiment, observing my own kind, keeping them at arm's length, so that I can get a better picture of the country I left behind. The glorious nation! I realise that if it was not for Alicja – less so my parents – I probably would not have anybody to go back to. I am talking here about my family, not the cannabis business of course, about which I am still to tell you. I almost have to force a feeling of enthusiasm every time I make the decision to travel back home. Even now I have second thoughts about this trip but, as I told you, I had no choice.

In those early days I reasoned that once I was back in our country a feeling of belonging would somehow work its way through my mind, instead of fighting with perpetual ferocity the connection with my birthplace and its people. But helplessness, more than anything, engulfed me every time I thought about visiting Poland. It was, and still is, a love-hate relationship. Perhaps I am prejudiced, fixated on finding faults rather than trying to understand where I came from, but travelling back and forth unveiled my hostility which, in the end, overshadowed any positives in my idea of this country.

With the new job now confirmed I decided to fly to Warsaw to visit Alicja. I had a few weeks before I started. I asked Jerome to come and water the plants I grew in the basement, the Jamaican Sensi, and feed the plants at the aeroponics garden, while I was away. It was only for a short weekend but I did not want to take the chance of coming back to find out the plants had suffered in any way. I would never forgive myself for that.

Now, I have not mentioned it so far but Jerome and I had become business partners. Initially he supplied me with the cuttings before I began to take them myself from the plants I grew. You see, you cannot run an operation like that on your own. Jerome is my confidante, the only person I trust with the growing and distribution. We both developed it to the global network it is now. My business is divided between two places: London flats where I grow special strains for my most devoted clients, and myself of course, and Poland, with its underground bunkers and open air crop. Now, I would not smoke the aeroponics myself. Piotrek, my Polish business partner – I will tell you in detail later – feeds them with blood and bone-meal. Not my kind of thing. I prefer to smoke cannabis grown in dirt. Ah, the taste in your mouth, the richness of earthy flavours filling your lungs with every inhalation, the way your tongue wraps around the smoke in your mouth, trying to distinguish the individual components of that very particular plant. I guess it is a personal preference when it comes to taste. Still, the aeroponics gives quicker yields of the crop, which is the core basis of my sales in the UK.

I think I have diverted from my story. Let me go back to what I was saying. The trip to visit my sister.

Alicja, her immaculate black dress tightly wrapped around her slim body, was waiting in the arrival hall of Frederic Chopin Airport. Her long blond hair, which her hairdresser who boasted celebrity clients took great care of, was loosely held back. She was wearing a little blue scarf that I had posted to her for her last birthday knotted around her throat. I saw her before she saw me. I suddenly remembered how much I missed the physical proximity of her body, inhaling perfume from her wrist when she stroked my cheek, being able to touch her straightened hair, looking at the tiny wrinkles around her eyes when she was arguing with me. I waited until the tears choking my throat subsided and walked towards her.

'Have you told the parents you are coming?' she asked, after we greeted each other and she was now leading me to her car. She put her arm through mine, gently squeezing me as we walked side by side.

'No.'

We sat in the car and I opened the glove compartment in search of a lighter. 'I came to see you. Besides, you know I can't talk about all this with them. They wouldn't understand it.' She snorted and asked me to light a cigarette for her while she concentrated on driving.

'What do you fancy? Do you want to stay at home or go out?'

'Let's go home first and then decide what to do,' I replied, looking out through the window at the people we were passing. Two girls were kissing on the lips, one of them kept her hand behind the other's head. An older woman who was passing them by lowered her gaze and shook her head in disapproval. I remember thinking how brave they were to do it in the open. Was it because we were in Warsaw? Was it a sign of change? Elderly people had their faces contracted in seriousness and sadness.

'Are you all right?' she asked, briefly turning her head to glance at me.

'Of course,' I said, focusing on my own face reflected in the window in front of me.

She looked in the rear-view mirror and carefully applied red lipstick when we stopped at the lights.

'You look tired,' I said. Her undereyes were puffy but her make up was impeccable. She put the car in first gear and said, 'You should see yourself.'

'Is Krzysiek at home?'

'Not yet. He'll be in later tonight. He had to stay in the office and finish a contract with a client. He should be back home around nine.'

On the way home we stopped at Carrefour to buy food. Alicja rarely had anything to eat in the fridge, and if she did it was almost certain to be past its expiry date. She said she was too busy to worry about food shopping, often leaving the office late in the evenings, too tired to fight her way among the shelves. Besides, she was never a big eater. She was fixated on keeping her figure slim. 'It's Warsaw, you know the pressure to look good, you should see the women in my office,' she said, as if embarrassed that I had mentioned she almost looked too skinny and there was nothing attractive about her collar bones sticking out through her blouse.

In the shop she disappeared among the shelves while I stood in front of the cheese section, starring stupidly at the display. The prices were higher every time I went to Poland and some products cost as much as, or more than, they did in London. Of course the prices in the capital were higher than the rest of the country; still, I was intrigued by how ordinary people could afford to live on their salaries, which were in most cases a fraction of what I was making in London. Alicja did not think that there was something obscene about the prices of the individual products and the money people haemorrhaged on food. She did not have to think because she was a corporate lawyer. She was used to buying whatever she wanted. I think in a way she was making up for the time when we did not have enough food during our childhood.

When Alicja and I were growing up in communist Poland, in the early eighties, the most basic products were rationed. If they were not rationed, there was next to nothing in the shops anyway; the true bliss of a socialist state. Why worry about food, if we lived in the happiest and most peaceful place on the planet, under the watchful and caring eyes of Uncles Stalin and Lenin?

Luckily for you, you don't have to worry about it now. There is plenty of everything now.

We lived on the fourth floor in a block of flats, opposite a huge complex of buildings which the Soviet army took over after 1945. The Soviets occupied them until the 1990s. After they left the buildings, they burnt and looted everything they could get their hands on. It was heartbreaking to see the devastation that came with their departure.

We used to come to the gates surrounding the Soviet military buildings trying to find a way to sneak into the sweet shops on the army's premises. The Soviet soldiers were well catered for. Most of the high-ranking officers were transferred to Poland with their large families. They were provided with schools, hospitals and shops. Bearing in mind there was almost nothing in the Polish shops, it made sense for the Soviets to have their own, where they could easily buy whatever they needed.

As children, we usually went there as a group of five or six. One or two would try to get in, while the rest waited anxiously outside for the two children to come back with pockets full of sweets, cookies, and a product that resembled chocolate. We did not know what real chocolate tasted like because we did not have it in the shops.

Standing there in the middle of the shop I recalled our first trip across the border to Erfurt in the Deutsche Demokratische Republik, where our aunt lived. This sudden childhood memory made me think how much my country had changed. How much we had changed. How easily we got used to things we never knew existed.

'Go on. Pick whatever you want,' my aunt encouraged. She was my father's younger sister and she had married a German, which in itself was enough to give a heart attack to my maternal grandmother, a concentration camp survivor. Our grandmother rarely spoke about the time during the war. But our grandfather always told the same story, how together with my grandmother they dug a tunnel and sprinkled black pepper so that the German shepherds would not sniff them out. I wasn't convinced the story was true but that was the only thing they told Alicja and me about their time in the concentration camps. Perhaps it was better not to know the truth. We learnt enough during the school trips to Auschwitz-Birkenau. I know you haven't been there yet but one day I think you should go.

And so, our aunt, who quickly got used to living abroad, perhaps forgot Alicja and I had no idea that chocolate bars could be so big. We were looking around the display of shapes and wrapping papers which screamed in reds, yellows and blues, terrified by the choice we were face to face with. We did not know what to do.

'Quickly!' she said. Alicja and I kept staring wide eyed and with our mouths open. 'We haven't got all the time. We still need to do some shopping.'

'Don't be shy. You can have anything you want,' my mother said and pushed us towards a display counter.

Yes, there was something that caught my eye. It was a stack of what looked like flat coins, each wrapped in golden paper with a face of Napoleon.

I pointed my finger, 'This is what I want.'

Alicja, who was standing next to me with her eyes firmly set in front of her, nodded her head in agreement and we squeezed our hands to give each other courage.

'Are you sure?' my aunt asked with a mocking smile lingering at the edges of her lips.

I said yes.

They all started laughing at us together with a stocky shop assistant. Holding hands, Alicja and I looked at each other.

Why did they laugh at us? I remember feeling ashamed. I think Alicja was too.

'They are sold by weight you silly!' my aunt said, and nodded at the shop assistant who grabbed a handful of coins between her fingers which looked like Frankfurter sausages and placed them in two bags to weigh.

Two bags brimming with coins with Napoleon's face landed into our trembling hands, and all of a sudden, Alicja and I wanted to disappear. What were we supposed to do with them now? We could eat them for years to come. We were terrified of what would happen at the border on the way back home after somebody discovered we were carrying bags full of golden coins with Napoleon's face on each of them. Not only were they colourful and shiny, which back in our grey and gloomy country would make us highly visible, but you always had to be vigilant not to draw attention to yourself, especially at school. Always beware of the individualistic and decadent Western inclinations! More importantly there was a face of a revolutionary on each coin. What kind of message would it send to the children at school, with whom we would surely share our treasure? Well, I did not want to but Alicja saved hers, and when we returned I saw her sharing chocolate with other children at school. And she did that for free! Yes, I was never good at giving things for free; you could almost forget we were sisters. Whatever I give comes with a price tag.

'What are you thinking about?' Alicja's question suddenly brought me back to the present.

'Do you remember the chocolate coins we got, when we visited Aunt Lucyna in Germany? You know, the ones with Napoleon's face?'

'Oh, yes. God! It was a long time ago. Seems like a lifetime. Have you decided what you want?' she asked, and not waiting for me to answer, quickly asked the shop assistant for a selection of cheeses, pointing at the ones she wanted. Just like our aunt.

'I think I want to keep this new job.'
'I was asking about the cheese.'

Alicja and Krzysiek's five-bedroom apartment was located in a well kept and fully-guarded green neighbourhood, in Praga Poludnie borough, on the east bank of the Wisla river. Each room was immaculately designed, with almost surgical precision, like a snapshot from a glossy magazine. Even the fresh flowers in the vases in each room matched either the colour of the walls or the colour of the furniture. The place was flawless. I wondered when she found the time to do it, but then I remembered she hired one of those very expensive interior designers.

The Ukrainian cleaning woman was still inside when we got in. She was finishing up, hiding the vacuum cleaner in a closet, and helped Alicja with the shopping bags.

'Thank you, Svetlana,' Alicja said in Russian without a trace of a Polish accent. 'You can go home now and I will see you on Tuesday.'

I do not remember much Russian although it was obligatory at school. It is a language I suppressed over the years, unlike Alicja. But wait, there is one socialist song we sang fervently during academias, which drilled its way into my memory: 'Let there always be a sun / Let there always be the sky / Let there always be mummy / Let there always be me.' The rest is about the peace that the people of the socialist states want. We also sang about the brave Soviet soldiers who liberated the Poles from Nazi occupation.

The teachers made us wear red scarves around our necks and lapel pins with the Soviet flag. Alicja was a diligent student and managed to learn Russian despite the hatred towards the language. Now, I envied her because she could read Fyodor Dostoyevsky, Alexander Solzhenitsyn or Mikhail Bulgakov in the original, whereas I read them in Polish translations.

You don't learn Russian at school any more, do you? I think it is English, German and French now.

'Is that a new girl?' I asked, when the cleaning lady left the apartment. 'What happened to Elena?'

'She had to go back to Ukraine. Svetlana is much better. More thorough,' Alicja said and went to the kitchen to open a bottle of wine she had bought in the shop. She poured two glasses and handed me one. We installed ourselves on the sofa in the living room. There were bookshelves opposite us with rows of neatly assembled legal volumes. On one of the walls hung a tribal Kota mask made of wood and sheet copper. Krzysiek had brought it back from his trip to the Congo.

At the end of the second bottle of wine, Krzysiek returned home. Without taking his coat off, he walked into the living room and hugged me closely. Alicja cast a reluctant glance at his shoes. The last thing she wanted were wet patches on their mahogany wood floor, shipped in from Canada. It was raining outside.

'I totally forgot it was today you were coming,' he said. 'I'm so sorry I'm so late. I would've come back home earlier.' He kissed me affectionately on my cheek, wrapping his arms around my body in a tight grip. He smelled faintly of cigarette smoke.

'No problem,' I said. 'It was out of the blue.' I tried to release myself from his warm hands. He went to the kitchen and brought a glass for himself.

'Let me guess. You pissed somebody off in London.' Krzysiek laughed, sitting heavily next to Alicja. He slid an arm around her shoulder and wanted to kiss her lips but she turned her head and his mouth touched her cheek instead. Krzysiek leaned across the table and poured himself some wine. He took a gulp to hide the shadow of sourness which flashed across his face.

'You know me too well,' I said. 'How's the business?'

'Couldn't be better.'

'Are you still working on that project with Ernst &Young?'

'We finished it last week.' He drank more wine, keeping his eyes on mine. 'We actually have a new one now with one of the major Swiss banks. That's why I had to stay a bit longer tonight.' He put a piece of Gruyère cheese in his mouth. 'Did Alicja tell you about the trip we are doing?' he mumbled. A small piece of cheese was stuck to his upper lip.

'No?'

'We're going to Chile for three weeks next year. I can't wait,' he said, and wiped his mouth with the back of his hand. The piece of cheese was now stuck to his hand.

'You know him,' Alicja said. She carefully placed crumbs of cheese which fell on the table back on the cheese board. 'He doesn't really need me there. The real reason for this trip is to take photos for his new photo album.' She wiped her hands with a paper napkin and handed him one to clean his hands. He put it aside on his thigh.

'Are you publishing a new one?' I asked. 'Didn't you publish one on Tibet last year?'

'He's got too much time on his hands. These albums are his babies,' Alicja said. 'Another bottle of the same or something else?'

'I don't mind,' I said.

'Sweetheart, why don't you get this Australian Cabernet I bought last week, you know, I think it might be still in the bag. I haven't had time to unwrap it,' Krzysiek said and added in my direction, 'Coming back to the albums, Tibet was last year but I'm ready to start working on a new one.'

Standing, Alicja handed the new bottle to Krzysiek who poured the wine into three fresh glasses.

'What's the news on you trying to have a baby?' I asked.

Alicja sat down, lit a cigarette, exhaled the smoke through her mouth and said, 'We decided to go to Switzerland to try IVF. It's almost impossible to do it here.'

'Is it really that bad?' I asked and tried the new wine. 'It's quite good.' I smacked my lips.

'Let me try,' said Alicja and took a big gulp. She nodded her head in approval. 'Well done, babe.'

'Thank you,' he said. 'The Church has made a new proposal to Parliament. The law will punish gynaecologists, GPs, anyone who helps people to get in-vitro but not the parents. The Catholic media are calling for three years' imprisonment for doctors. They call in-vitro a "sophisticated abortion." All the doctors are scared. Do you remember the case of Alicja Tysiac?'

'The one who won the case against the government in Strasbourg?' I said. Krzysiek nodded his head.

'The European Court of Human Rights awarded her twenty five thousand Euros in damages after she was refused an abortion, although she had the legal right to it under abortion law,' he said.

Alicja leaned forward and cut the air with her flat palms. 'We thought something would change. Perhaps we need more women like her.'

Alicja was spiritual, though not in the ferocious way my mother was. My sister tortuously navigated her life in Poland between what the Catholic Church expected from her as a devoted member, and what she, as a woman, deemed practical and necessary. I kept a safe distance from the Church.

'It makes you wonder, though, that we are a member of the European Union,' I said.

'What did you expect? It is Catholic fundamentalism. Different methods, same objective,' Krzysiek said in a loud voice.

'I am glad you said it, not me,' I added quickly. It felt so good being with them.

'But it is true!' Alicja joined in. 'All this talk about Muslim fundamentalism in the press and television but nobody says that right in the heart of Europe Catholic fundamentalists are quietly gaining more and more power. And your abortion?'

'It was a long time ago.'

I was turning a wine glass in my hand wondering how much it was my decision or my mother's, who used her savings to pay the doctor. To this day my father has never found out what happened. I wonder how my mother has kept it secret all these years.

I want you to know that I have no regrets that I did it. I forgive the person I was when it happened to me. Then, there was overpowering guilt in her, haunted by the fear she, or her mother, would go to prison. She was seventeen, sitting among other women in the doctor's surgery and guessing how many women might be there to do the same thing. She and her mother avoided each other's eyes, looking at some magazine pages spread on their knees, not reading the words or seeing the black and white photos, waiting to be called in by the nurse. I remember she was scared, glancing towards the door, thinking what if the police stormed in and arrested her and her mother. How would she explain herself? Would they arrest her mother? Would they come after her sister? Even when she was sitting with her legs in the stirrups, the entry to her private parts on display, she was petrified somebody would come in. Shame engulfed her throughout the whole procedure until it gave way to a huge feeling of relief. It was gone. Only emptiness in her lower abdomen. Thanks to her, I am free now.

I blame everybody for what led to that; the school which, instead of sexual education, employed a priest who told us that life was the most precious gift from God and that sex was only about procreation; my mother who was too ashamed to talk to me about contraception; the gynaecologist who said I was too young to have sex so I did not need anything to protect myself. I blame this country, which failed me, installing backward religious teachings instead of helping me, terrorizing women and doctors into submission.

And now, sixteen years later, abortion is still illegal, sexual education almost nonexistent, and the country goes on a witch-hunt after gynaecologists who feel sorry for women with unwanted pregnancies. It is a sad country to live in.

I do not think Alicja ever came to terms with my abortion. I say she was lucky. The choice between education or motherhood was almost irreconcilable to her and she was relieved she never had to face such a decision. Perhaps because Alicja was caught between the teachings of the Catholic Church and her personal rights which were so easily curbed by the Catholic obligations. At least she refrained from moralizing about the past now. I never doubted that education came first. And at the age of seventeen I did not see myself as fit to embrace motherhood. I did not want to think where I would be if I had not made that decision then. You and I would probably never have met. Who knows?

'Are you still in touch?' Krzysiek asked.

'With whom?'

'The father of your child, of course.'

'He had nothing to do with it,' I said. I was surprised he had brought my unborn child's father into this conversation. Apart from Alicja nobody knew the details of my past, and I certainly did not want Krzysiek to put me on the stand now. 'I don't see the point in talking about him.'

'I'm sorry,' he added. 'I didn't mean to.'

Krzysiek poured more wine into our glasses, and I said, 'I remember looking for a doctor when Marzena got pregnant. We ended up on the outskirts of Wroclaw, in a private house. There was no nurse and the place looked like a slaughterhouse. I mean, it wasn't, but something didn't feel right about the whole set up. There was a light bulb hanging on a wire from the ceiling, which didn't give enough light and we sat in semi darkness. The linoleum floor was covered with footprints. And worst of all, we both detected a distinctive sour smell of alcohol. That was enough for us. We ran away from there after fifteen minutes. It didn't take us long to make that decision. And then Marzena found a gynaecologist, a private practice. It was a huge gamble because we didn't know whether he would report us. The deal was sealed in a few sentences: "You are five weeks pregnant." "Oh." "Do you want to keep the baby?" "Is there anything you can do?" "Are you sure?" "Yes." "I will schedule appointment at the hospital." And that was it. He told her the price. And the next week, it was done.'

'At least he admitted her to the hospital and fabricated paperwork,' Alicja said. 'You were both very lucky. Everybody is so terrified these days.'

'We exchanged red flags for black cassocks,' Krzysiek added.

'Apparently around ten thousand Polish women come to the UK to terminate unwanted pregnancies,' I said. 'And supposedly ninety per cent of Poles are Catholics, right? So tell me, is religion in this country a farce, or as a nation are we simply cowards whipped by the rosaries?'

Krzysiek stood up and brought a second bottle of Cabernet from the kitchen. While twisting the corkscrew into the cork, he said, 'There should be a referendum about it.'

'Have you ever thought about a political career?' I said, winking at him and blowing him a kiss on my right palm.

'And Pope John Paul II?' Alicja said suddenly, her voice unsteady, slurring the words. 'If I got raped, I wouldn't want to keep the child. And he forbade the use of condoms!' She was almost shouting now.

I thought she must be drunk now because she would never allow herself to oppose the dead Pope when sober. She knew too well how the public reacted to such comments. I had never heard her speak like that before. She would never criticize the Pope in front of our parents, or anybody else.

'I wish your mother could hear both of you now,' Krzysiek commented.

'So what's the situation with IVF? You said you were going to Switzerland,' I changed the topic.

'Alicja is about to start taking hormones, and we are due to visit the doctors at the end of this month.' Krzysiek leaned and briefly kissed her on her lips. She didn't like it when he showed her affection, even in front of me. Our parents rarely displayed their feelings in front of us when we were children. In this respect, Alicja was similar to my mother who rebuked my father when his lips came close to her face.

'And what if you don't get pregnant?' I asked.

'I will,' Alicja stated firmly, as if simply by saying it aloud she would ensure all would go according to plan. She did not accept the idea that something would not work in her carefully planned life.

'We're going to adopt,' Krzysiek said and I looked in surprise at him. I wondered about his trips to remote lands. How was he going to justify fatherhood in his life? Was he serious about adopting or was it a way of keeping my sister occupied, to avoid guilt when he left her in Poland while he disappeared for weeks?

Alicja leaned towards me and said, 'Magda, we have all this money and what? You know I always wanted to be a mother and maybe I shouldn't have waited so long. I'm over thirty now. I wanted to be successful and achieve something, for myself. You know what I'm saying, make a difference?' She hesitated, looking for my acceptance of the life decisions in which she rarely involved me.

Was she ready to have her perfect life turned upside down? She knew my opinion about motherhood and the last thing she needed was my permission. I wanted to prove I could be as successful as she was, but I was not going to compete with her over who got pregnant first. I knew she would succeed. She always did.

'And it is great, don't get me wrong' she said. 'I have achieved everything that I – that we – wanted,' she corrected herself, and briefly looked at Krzysiek but he was not looking at her as his eyes were set on mine, 'but we want a family now. Right, sweetheart?' She placed her hand on his knee. Krzysiek was leaning against the sofa and Alicja sat at the edge. She had to turn her head and torso to see his face. That was why she did not see him staring at me all that time while she was talking about the baby. And I was carefully gazing into her eyes, not wanting to invite his attention. 'It's what we dream about,' she finished. She removed her hand from his knee.

'Of course, of course,' Krzysiek said. He did not sound convincing to me.

'I never told you how happy I am you have come,' Alicja said. She stood up and came over to me to touch my hair. 'I like it short.'

'Do you ever think about coming back?' Krzysiek asked. 'You can always stay with us, until you find something for yourself.'

A few years back I would have been touched by his offer, but not now.

'There's nothing to come back to. Nothing.'

It was two o'clock in the morning and I helped Alicja take the glasses and plates of uneaten cheese to the kitchen. Krzysiek had already placed my luggage in the spare room where I was going to sleep. She said good night and went to their bedroom. I heard water running in the bathtub.

As I left the guest bathroom I saw Krzysiek outside in the corridor.

'How long have you been standing here?' I asked. I could not think of a reason why he would wait for me in the middle of the night.

'I can't sleep,' he said.

'I'm going to bed. I'm exhausted and drunk.'

He came closer and slid his hands under the towel I was wrapped in and kissed me on my lips.

'Are you out of your mind?' I asked, and stepped back.

'Alicja is already asleep.'

'You're drunk.'

'I wanted to see what it was like. If I still remember your taste.'

'I don't have time for this now.'

On Saturday we went to the Old Town and stopped in one of the cafés. While Alicja and I discussed our parents and the future of her pregnancy, Krzysiek visited a shop with old maps. He returned one hour later with a bulky package under his arm. It was an 18th century map of Warsaw he wanted to frame and hang on one of the empty walls in the corridor. Alicja was not pleased when she saw what he had bought. She said it would not go with the design of the apartment. 'Unless you want to sacrifice one of your African masks,' she suggested. There was a tension between them I had not noticed before. I wondered if Alicja had heard our conversation outside the bathroom or, worse, had seen us kissing, but I thought it was better not to ask.

We walked the streets of central Warsaw. Although it was the weekend it was deserted except for a few vendors sitting on folded chairs with their eclectic merchandise displayed on crates in front of them: second-hand books, matryoshka dolls, woollen mittens, Soviet stars and flag badges, buttons for the military coats. Perhaps it was the weather; the cold east wind brought headaches if you walked too long with your head uncovered. I used to think that Warsaw was crowded. The city seemed almost too spacious, with not enough inhabitants to fill its streets, the facades of concrete buildings covered in advertisements. An unwelcoming walk down the main streets.

We passed the famous Blikle patisserie on Nowy Swiat where we bought doughnuts with rose petal marmalade, and Florentynki almond cookies. I told them that I was meeting old friends and would see them at home. 'Don't wait for me to have dinner. I'll probably come back home late,' I said. I stood on the pavement, watching as their car drove away when I hailed the taxi.

The things about having your own business is that you always work. Do you remember the boys I told you about, the ones I smoked weed in the park behind the high school building? Now, most of them had ended up with office jobs in Warsaw banks, consultancy agencies, married, their children attending private schools, their wives heading their own companies, basically leading uneventful and boring lives.

Luckily for me, not all of them.

Piotrek was nothing like the rest who were interested in recreational smoking; he wanted to grow, like me. You see, as I said earlier, you need people, you can't do everything yourself, especially if you do it in many locations.

'The equipment is ready,' he said when I arrived at his flat. He laid out a plan on the table with the plot in eastern Poland. He tapped his finger at the map. 'Pumps, high-pressure spray heads, hoses. I will need more cash for the lamps.'

'What were you thinking of getting?'

'Metal halide.'

'Okay. We can start with that but I'd prefer sodium vapour. Let's see how they will grow. How many tubes?'

'Ten, twenty plants each.'

'Make it eight. That will give us one hundred and sixty plants. Enough for now.'

'You're the boss.'

'Have you started digging?'

'Next month.'

'What about the generator?'

'All in place. I meant to ask you, who is going to be our distributor for the UK?'

'Don't worry about that. Get everything ready.'

One underground shipping container, roughly ten to twelve crops a year, each crop worth half a million pounds.

Now we are talking!

It was just before midnight when I let myself into Alicja and Krzysiek's flat. I heard their voices coming from their bedroom. I passed their door without knocking and went to my room to get ready for my flight the next day.

The flight was scheduled for two in the afternoon on Sunday. I was flying with BA and I did not have to worry about the weight of my luggage, filled as it was with books, magazines, newspapers and cigarettes. I had bought three cartons and Alicja gave me another two. The cigarettes I bought while visiting my family were less than half the price that I paid in London.

The UK government is ever so eager to punish people for smoking. I do not terrorise people on the streets or force them to inhale and die. I do not preach that smoking cigarettes is healthier than stuffing your face with hamburgers and junk food. Is the UK government really serious about stopping people smoking? How about all the money they make on taxing tobacco? I am telling you this whole crusade against smokers makes me sick. Really, really sick. Have you read this highly inventive stuff they write on cigarette packets? 'Choose freedom, we'll help you.'

Yeah, right. I've already made my choice, so leave me the fuck alone!

I'm sorry about the swearing. It's her, not me. Sometimes I hate myself for what she makes me say to you. Where was I? Ah, smoking.

Once I was walking down a railway platform near my house. A fellow passenger, a woman in her late twenties, walking right next to me said, 'You are so brave.'

'Excuse me?'

'You know. Smoking,' she indicated a cigarette in my fingers. 'It's forbidden.'

'What do you think they are going to do? Arrest me in the middle of the night for smoking on a platform?'

'But they have cameras. They can see you. Don't get me wrong, I admire your courage.'

I wish people admired me for something else, not for lighting a cigarette on a deserted platform in the middle of the night.

I looked at her with pity in my eyes, 'Do you always do what the state tells you to do? Be brave! Surprise yourself!' And I added, quoting Barack Obama, 'Yes, you can!'

I checked my luggage in and Alicja and I went outside the airport to have a last smoke. The wind briefly lifted the silk scarf around her neck and she held it with her hand.

'When are you going to visit me next?' she asked, wrapping the scarf tighter.

'When was the last time you flew to London to visit me?'

Since I had left Poland Alicja had never visited me in London. During the first few months she provided me with innocent explanations. Later I stopped asking her. I explained to myself that it was her way to make sure I would come back.

'Maybe after we get back from Switzerland. I really would like to get going with the IVF.' We both knew she wouldn't come.

'Well, I'll keep my fingers crossed for you and Krzysiek. I would love you to come, any time you want. Listen, I didn't want to ask at home but is he serious?'

'Serious about what?'

'Being a father?'

'Why?'

'I want you to be sure this is what you both want.'

'Of course he's serious. Is there something I should know? Something you're not telling me?' She looked at me intently. I noticed how perfect her make-up was.

'No,' I answered and hugged her so that she would not see my eyes. We stood holding each other for a while.

'I will miss you,' she whispered. Her breath tickled my ear.

'Now, go back home. My plane leaves in forty-five minutes. I better go back inside.'

'I love you,' she said suddenly, still holding her arms around me.

'I love you, too.' I lifted my bag and walked towards the airport building.

I wanted to look back but she did not let me, making my feet move steadily, taking me away from my sister.

On the plane I could not wait to land in London. The weekend visit to Warsaw already seemed like an unreal event, an abstract reality. What mattered to me was now, my plants and a new cover job. If I was not meeting Piotrek to discuss cannabis production or the lawyer to establish a legal infrastructure which involved making hemp-based products and distributing them around Europe, I was planless. I filled the days with my sister's life. When I was not spending time with my sister or my clients I was engulfed in a feeling of emptiness. I had nothing else to do. I was unable to define the visits to Poland. Holidays? Coming back home? It was none of those things. I had become a visitor in other people's lives. I used to mean something. Even the lives of the friends I left behind raised little concern in me. My clients? For them I had become a reliable supplier of the highest quality cannabis.

Back at my London house I dropped the bag on the floor and, without taking my coat off, I went to the basement where I grew weed. The lights were still on. I breathed, relieved. I still had around half an hour before the timer automatically switched the lights off. After that I would not be able to go inside the room. I inspected the plants. They had enough water in their pots. Jerome had left me a note on the small table where I kept gardening tools, scissors, gloves, a watering can and bottles of organic fertilizer. 'Look under the leaves. Spider mite infestation?' I kneeled next to the plant closest to me and gently twisted each leaf. I could not find anything and I sighed with relief. I looked at the second plant. Then I saw them. Tiny, white crawling dots, under the leaves. I looked closer and saw a very delicate web between individual twigs. Not good. And I did not have enough time before the timer switched the lights off in the room. I took out as many plants as I could. Outside the garden room I called Jerome.

'You were right. Tell me what to do,' I said.

'Isolate all the sick plants. Mix one to one pure alcohol with water and wipe each leaf. If you can soak them in water in a bathtub, upside down, or spray them, it should kill the spider mites.'

'It must be from the cuttings I got from Andreas.'

'Possibly. Do you want me to come over?' he asked. We would probably end up having sex but I wanted to get rid of the bugs so I said no.

'Okay. Call me if you need help.'

You see, that was my first lesson. When you bring cuttings from other people into your own garden there is a danger of bug or spider infestation. And the soil, of course. You must be careful with the type of the dirt you use. It is best to buy organic dirt and limit the exposure to various germs, bugs, worms and caterpillars that may be hibernating in there. The moisture and temperature make it the perfect environment for those nasties to wake up.

Andreas has been my constant and reliable supplier of cuttings and seeds for the past few years. I met him through Jerome and I trust him. Now I make my own cuttings from the plants I grow but at times I need to experiment with other strains. Andreas is Dutch and thanks to him I have access to competition weed. Once a year, in November, the Cannabis

Cup is held in Amsterdam. Andreas, Jerome and I meet at the venue in Amsterdam as travelling together can be too risky. That is how I got Black Widow and White Widow but what I grow now is mostly Cheese. It is the most popular strain among my clients, especially among the City workers. It is a milder smoke and the City workers do not like Jamaican Sensi, a much stronger and harsher strain which is popular among my West Indians clients. Jerome sells most of my Jamaican Sensi production.

I have not told you much about my clients because I still don't know if you will come back with me to London after the funeral. If you do, I would like you to get involved eventually in the business. It has been growing quite nicely, not without problems, mind you. I could use a reliable pair of hands. We have started planning for three more underground containers. You could learn so much from Piotrek.

Now that I think of it you could be my perfect legal front. At the moment it is only me who deals with the lawyer I mentioned earlier. I do not involve anybody else. Piotrek is a good worker on the ground but the legal front of keeping my production clean I leave in the hands of the professionals. Besides, the lawyer, who I reward well for his services and silence, knows exactly which customs officer, policeman or judge to buy. Yes, everybody has a price. We all want to live a better life. If it involves looking the other way or directing the attention of the sniffer dogs to somebody else's vehicle when the cars transporting cannabis cross the border, it is ultimately a small request in exchange for a generous flow of wads of bills. It's human nature. Money usually does the business, threats less so. Still, from time to time you find a staunch believer in the letter of law, but there is hardly anybody who would not do anything to protect their family. A small threat to the lives of others usually gives me what I want. But, you do not have to worry about that side of the business. It will not be your concern, not in the beginning at least.

Crime is a risk analysis, and I reward generously for protection. Loyalty, even if bought, is a powerful ally.

Now, let's leave the story about my clients for later. I know you would like to hear about them but first things first. I promise I will come back to that.

That day I took care of all the sick plants.

The next day I started my new cover job in the Department of Health as an assistant to Campbell, a civil servant, head of the project. The rumour was that if he was successful he could become a minister one day.

I had never worked in the public sector before, let alone a government department. Walking every day on Whitehall, between the Cabinet Office and Ministry of Defence, before entering the swing door that leads into the Department of Health, opposite the Foreign Office, had a certain appeal; it gave me a feeling of belonging, of being one of the few who could make a difference in society. I thought my mother would be proud of me, but instead she only asked me how long it would be before I antagonised somebody and moved to work somewhere else. So I told her lying stories that this time everything would be different. It was the first job of which Alicja wholeheartedly approved.

I must say there was also another, more enticing, element to my working for the British government. You see, unfortunately it is still illegal to sell weed in the UK and I thought that this new job offered me a nice cover. After I passed all the security checks I was pleased that the British secret services deemed me a good citizen, worthy of being trusted to work in public service. Sweet!

I joined a group of three other assistants; Jackie, Shanice and Susan. Each of us was responsible for a different aspect of Campbell's life. Jackie, thirty-something, Oxford educated, was in charge of press and contact with the MPs. She was the longest serving assistant in the team. The joke among the women was that you could only work for Campbell for five months. After that you were either unceremoniously made redundant or you resigned, if you wanted to keep your sanity. Shanice's responsibilities covered contacts with the clients and contractors. She had the bubbliest personality and her hearty laugh would often defuse the tense atmosphere in the office. Conferences, public appearances and the calendar of events landed on my desk. Susan, the team leader, was the quietest of all, rarely participating in telling jokes in the office. She always spoke with the authority her position demanded.

I was glad for their friendship as by then I had lost touch with Lorraine. I was disappointed, especially after what we had been through. I heard that she kept working in the telecom company for a few more weeks after I was gone, but she soon resigned, unable to face Neville every day. She did not want to keep in touch and I did not press her at first. Eventually she stopped answering my emails or phone calls. Did she refuse to speak to me because I brought back bad memories of the time we spent together in the telecom company? Her silence towards me made me doubt that she ever thought of me as a friend.

So much for friendship.

Of course, life being what it is, I moved on. As I said earlier, I rarely form emotional attachments to people. It is easier that way.

Although I relished in the daily dealings with the women, peppered with jokes about Campbell when he was out of earshot, over months I witnessed the way he skilfully allocated taxpayers' money between government projects and his private life. He believed he was irreplaceable and invincible; a superman of the public services. Campbell had almost unlimited access to government funding, and he had the right to direct part of the money to make his and his family's life comfortable. His wife and three children lived in the Lake District to which he commuted every Friday to stay over the weekend. It was not unusual for Campbell to claim expenses for all the construction jobs, gardening, cleaning and babysitters, together with his wife's travel expenses for shopping trips while in London. And this came long before the MPs' expenses balloon burst a few years later. The joys of working in a government department!

I admit, what I do is illegal, according to British law. At least I provide my clients with a much needed respite from the mundanity of their lives. My weed saves lives! Actors, writers, musicians and traders cannot and will not work without my help. And what was Campbell doing in the Department of Health? Stealing public money and making lives even more miserable.

How I wanted to wipe the smirk off his face, how she wanted to make one phone call and end this farce. We both knew better than that.

'You may not like my style but in order to keep this circus in place, you need a tight grip. This job is not for the faint hearted,' he once said to me. 'Remember, you can leave at any moment,' he added, to clarify my options but I had already made up my mind.

He was right. Not my circus, not my monkeys. Who was I trying to fool? I was nobody. If it had been me in this position, would I be like him? Would I throw my morals out of the window? Patrick did not. I mistook Campbell's compulsion to make a difference in the public health-care system for genuine concern, but he was just another sucker for money and position. But then, aren't we all, in some way?

I did not know whether Campbell wanted me to leave because I was becoming noticeably disheartened or because he simply did not warm to my aloof personality. He may have heard my disgruntled comments while talking with the other women but I did not care anymore. Certainly, the longer I worked for him, the less respect I had left for him. He was a living legend among the circles of contractors, and much feared because of his political contacts. In my naïveté I believed I could make a difference, by working for the government on one of their biggest projects, intended to make the lives of all NHS patients across the UK easier. I think at that time I still had some ideals in life. True, all my jobs served their purpose, but that doesn't mean I couldn't try to make a difference where I worked. And where else if not working for the public services? But once again the reality slapped me across my face like a stinky fish tail, leaving a slimy film on my cheek. What did I expect?

This time it was Alicja who said to give him a chance, said that I needed to get to know him better, to understand that Campbell's position demanded sacrifices. I didn't want to believe that she was affected by his aura of authority which, to me, blinded her judgment. She was ready to forgive him because he occupied a position of influence. Now I think she was preparing me for a future forgiveness, if she chose to pursue a stand which required sacrifices. She wanted me to see the larger picture of a person caught in between personal beliefs, and expectations imposed by agents outside one's control. I refused to see Campbell that way.

Frustrated with the reality around me, disillusioned and resentful, I began to transform into a fully-fledged sore, an ulcer, ready to explode at a slightest touch. I began to see salt in everybody and everything, and developed a painfully joyful satisfaction in rubbing it on my insides till they started to burn.

And so it happened to me again, my contract was terminated. It was not working out, I was informed.

Somehow I felt relieved on the way back home after I had been removed from my duties. Not having to get up in the morning and see or hear Campbell seemed like a long-awaited blessing. Needless to say, Alicja did not hide her disappointment at the way my contract ended. She almost said she blamed me, but I quickly pointed out that it was his inappropriate behaviour which was to blame, not mine. Of course, I was confused by her reaction. I was unsure what she was asking me to do. Why was I supposed to put up with Campbell for the sake of keeping my employment? My sister only saw opportunity this employment could offer, but I was not interested in making a career in a government department, let alone torturing myself every day with a job I had no interest in.

It is late. I will let you sleep now. I will come back tomorrow. I promise. But now I have to talk to my parents and you need a rest. It's been a long day for both of us.

I still have to discuss the funeral arrangements, pay Father Maciej, the undertaker, the florist. We can't forget about the food for the wake, when the vultures – I mean the aunts and uncles – arrive to feed on the carcass of my family, fake some enthusiasm for helping out, gorge on our loss and pretend it is theirs. At least for now they leave us in peace so you and I can spend some time together before they come to you and offer their help. Don't trust them! Don't trust anybody. They will tell you things about me. Lies. That's why I want you to listen to me and remember everything I've said to you and will say.

You are the only person to whom I am telling the whole truth about myself. I hope with time you can forgive me.

But now you don't have to worry about anything. You can leave it up to me. I will take care of it. I am here to protect you from them.

four

ARE YOU ASLEEP? I know it's the middle of the night but I thought I would check whether you are okay.

All right, I am going to be honest with you. I could not fall asleep. I called Jerome and told him about you, what a wonderful listener you have been. He can't wait to meet you already. Not sure what to think about it. I never thought he would be so eager to get to know you. And he hasn't even seen you. Only some photos I had of you. He said we can both take care of you. I admit his comment has thrown me off balance.

That is all for tonight. I will let you get some rest. You deserve it. You have been a good listener so far. I must say I am impressed. And I have taken more of your time than I intended.

Good night.

five

MY BACK IS KILLING ME! I hope your bed was more comfortable than mine. This one night I decide to sleep in this house and now I can't move. I have asked my mother so many times to buy a proper mattress. 'If you don't like it you can stay in a hotel,' she says whenever I complain. What am I supposed to do? She does not want money from me; she does not want anything from me.

The beautiful morning sun today reminds me of the day I found out my sister was going to be a mother.

'I'm pregnant!' she announced on the phone. I was sitting in my garden smoking a spliff. It was almost a week after I lost the job in the government department. It was one of the rare blue-skied days, cold, but sitting with my face to the winter sun I felt content.

'I'm so happy for you! This is great news.'

'I know. I still can't believe it. It's an amazing feeling, Magda.' She gave a laugh, half embarrassed, afraid to show how important it was to her.

'What did the doctors say?' I asked.

'You know what they're like,' Alicja quickly dismissed my concern. 'They said it is too early to say whether I will keep it. But I need to be careful now.'

'No more cigarettes and alcohol.'

'Will you be coming to our parents' house for Christmas?'

'I haven't decided yet.'

'Please, you must come. Magda, for the last two years you have refused to show up for Christmas. And now you have lost another job. That makes another reason for you to come.'

Then she offered to buy me a ticket, which I thought a very bad idea. If she did I would have no choice but to go and spend Christmas with the whole family and listen to the endless questions and pitiful comments about being single and childless. I could already hear my mother's condescending voice: 'Your clock is ticking. You're not getting any younger.' But now, with Alicja pregnant, the focus would be on her. So perhaps, after all, it was not such a bad idea to go home for Christmas. It was true that, since I had moved out, I had avoided going to my parents' house for Christmas. Instead, I travelled to Jamaica or South Africa at Christmas time, which also gave me a good reason not to visit my family over the festive period. Okay, I admit, most of those trips were to meet other growers, find out the prices on the ground and assess whether I could establish a business relationship.

'And besides,' Alicja continued, 'if you stay in London you will be alone. Unless you have booked yourself a trip to the other side of the world again? Have you?'

When I told her I would come she let out a deep sigh of relief and I gulped nervously while tiny drops of sweat unexpectedly settled on my temple. Home, I thought in a panic. I was going back home for Christmas after two years of skilfully avoiding this trip. I had managed to escape seeing my mother all this time. Our communication was limited to lying emails about how well I was doing in London and brief telephone conversations which usually meant me listening to her repetitive monologues about the importance of doing something useful with my life. At that time she was a restless woman, desperate to give desirable direction to my life, despite that fact I had already made my choices. I had no idea then what my other self would make of this visit. Would she be able to survive the performance without further antagonising the family? Would she let me reconcile? I didn't know what to expect. I didn't want to think the worst.

On the first day I told you that the family is best loved from a distance. I stand by that. Now, with what I am going to tell you, you can judge for yourself.

The plane was bursting with crying toddlers and equally desperate mothers trying to calm them down. I closed my eyes and tried to imagine the last Christmas I spent with my parents but the screams sliced through my memories. There was no escape from these little bundles of joy, who surprised me with the ferocity of their tearful outrage. I hopelessly longed for silence. Relief from the cacophony came only when I rushed to leave the plane after we landed. Pulling my heavily worn travel bag, I rushed to the exit. I almost ignored mother and Alicja at the arrival lounge, confused by the mobs of families eagerly crowded, waiting for the remaining passengers.

'Hello, Mum,' I said and hugged her stiff body. Alicja squeezed my arm I placed around my mother's neck and gave me a warm look of encouragement, as if to make up for her cold welcome.

'Okay. Good to see you, too. Finally,' my mother said. A shadow crossed her face as she pulled away from me. 'Let's go. I need to pay for the parking ticket.'

'Dad and Krzysiek went to the shop to buy two carp,' Alicja explained when I asked about them.

I struggled to fish out a lighter from my pocket while we were walking towards the parking lot.

'Do you really have to smoke right now?' my mother asked sharply. 'You shouldn't be smoking around your pregnant sister.' Her lips were tight and pale. She set her gaze in front of her, carefully stepping in the dirtied snow.

'It's not as if I'm blowing the smoke in her face,' I said with a cigarette in my mouth.

My mother did not respond. When I drew the breath in, the frost bit inside my nostrils.

'I forgot how cold it can get here in December.'

'Huh.' My mother mumbled something in return.

My mother drove slowly although the road was black and with no ice. She was an impatient driver, swearing at other cars when somebody did not want to let her into the lane. It took us more than an hour to reach the house – the house we are now in.

A real live Christmas tree was standing in the living room by the window with various decorations hanging from its branches and twigs; small apples, cinnamon sticks, hand-made colourful paper chains, candies, thin and long like earrings, pine cones painted silver and shimmering angel hair. On top, a large star cut from cardboard and wrapped in silver foil. A plastic Christmas tree had replaced the real one when the parents spent Christmas on their own. Two fat carp were swimming in the bathtub, slowly coming towards the surface when I switched the light on in the bathroom.

'Who's going to kill them?' I asked, observing the fish swimming from one end of the bathtub to another. Alicja was looking over my shoulder.

'Mum, of course. Who else did you think?'

'Jakub!' we heard our mother's impatient voice from the kitchen. 'Bring me a hammer from the tool box to kill the carp, now that the girls are finally home. I need to start preparing the fish for tomorrow.'

'How about Krzysiek?' I asked Alicja.

'Oh, no,' she dismissed me with a giggle. 'He's too weak. Besides, Mum would never let anybody touch the carp,' she said seriously. We looked at each other and burst out laughing. Standing next to the bathtub with two carp awaiting their imminent execution, we shared a rare moment of Christmas gaiety for which I almost felt a deep longing.

But it was the rare honest laughter I shared with Alicja that I missed, not my presence at my parents' house for Christmas celebrations.

We were sitting in the living room watching television when, with a splash and a few thudding noises, my mother quickly stepped out of the bathroom. It didn't take her long to kill the first fish. She held a small yellow basin with the dead carp. Her hands were covered in blood and there were red splashes on her kitchen apron. A few minutes later, she emerged from the kitchen and placed fish scales in Alicja's and my hands.

'For good luck,' she said. 'So that you will never run out of money. Put them in your wallets.'

'Pagan belief,' muttered my father.

'If you want to share your thoughts with us, Jakub, you might want to consider speaking up,' my mother snapped.

'Nothing. I was just talking to myself.' He took cover in the *Guardian* I bought for him in the airport in London.

'I thought so,' she said. 'Kici-kici-kici.' My mother was calling the cat. 'Here you are.' She bent down and stroked the fur of a six year-old tomcat, Filip, although we often called him Mr Filipowski. Filip immediately started purring and wrapping his tail around her legs. 'I've got something for you as well, my sweetheart,' she spoke softly as if she was talking to a child. 'Look.' She kneeled down and extended her hand with a swim bladder on top of it.

'Gross.' Alicja twisted her face in disgust. 'What are you going to do when he leaves it somewhere in the house and it starts to rot?'

'He'll eat it, don't you worry about it.' She dismissed Alicja's concern with a wave of her hand. She stood with her hands curled in fists propped against her hips, watching as the cat ran away inside the house.

'Oh, God, I think I'm going to be sick.' Alicja covered her mouth with her hand and ran out.

While the carp had its belly cut open, with my mother methodically removing the internal organs into a separate bowl, Alicja was gagging in the bathroom.

'Christ. It stinks in there,' my sister said after she returned, heavily slumping on the sofa.

Mr Filipowski came back and jumped on a small coffee table in the kitchen intensely following my mother's hands, while she was cleaning the fish and cutting it into smaller pieces. I admired my mother's aptitude for multitasking. While she was preparing the fish, three different pots simmered on the gas at the same time. She had been cooking bigos for the last three days. The cabbage was soft now and different types of meat and sausages began to release their juices. When my mother went to the outside garden to get the vegetables from a wooden box, Alicja and I sneaked into the kitchen, armed with forks to try some of her cooking. The aroma of it filled the whole kitchen mixed with the smell of the raw fish, which she left covered with a kitchen cloth to prevent the cat from trying to nibble on it.

'Girls!' my mother entered the kitchen before we noticed.

We stood hovering at the pot, trying to hide the forks in our hands.

'I don't want you in the kitchen. You will eat it tomorrow, during Christmas Eve dinner.'

'Sorry.' We bent our heads to hide the grins. 'Would you like us to do anything?' Alicja asked. She was unusually quick to offer help and I almost held it against her that she did not give me any chance to impress my mother. And she knew I needed that. I needed to do at least one thing right.

'I'm perfectly capable of doing everything myself.'

It was a tradition in our family, for as long as I could remember, that my mother prepared all the Christmas dishes herself. When Alicja and I were children, she would say that we were too small, and after we grew up, she said we were too old to learn how to cook. Still, we learnt by observing her carefully whenever she mercifully let us into the kitchen. But no touching! My mother was like an orchestra conductor of pots, frying pans, wooden spoons and forks, and knives of various sizes.

'How about uszka for the beetroot soup?' Alicja said.

'Yesterday, I made one hundred. I am surprised you haven't seen them in the fridge.' And then, unexpectedly, taking pity on us, she added, 'Well, you could make pierogi with soft cheese.'

'Great,' I jumped at her proposal, faking my enthusiasm. I did not have anything else to do so I decided to direct my attention to helping with the preparations.

Mixing flour, eggs and milk, in a large bowl, Alicja was preparing dough for pierogi, while I placed my ingredients on the other side of the table: cottage cheese, mashed potatoes (mother had already made the mash, so thankfully I did not need to spend hours peeling the potatoes), onion, salt and black pepper. My mother rarely tolerated competition in the kitchen. She permitted me and Alicja to engage with the lower-level tasks because we were women. But even under her scrutinizing eyes she was ready to deliver her lectures when we made mistakes. No wonder my father and Krzysiek cleverly evacuated themselves from the vicinity of my mother. As a result of my mother's almost military occupation of the kitchen, my father developed very limited cooking skills. He often survived on scrambled eggs or chips when my mother went to visit our grandparents and he was left to cook for himself.

'Look at the mess you are making,' my mother said and briskly approached me. She grabbed the wooden spoon I was using for mixing cheese and potatoes from my hands. 'This is the way you should do it,' she said, mixing the ingredients the same way I had been doing so far, perhaps more vigorously. She then licked the wooden spoon. 'Too bland,' she pronounced her verdict, throwing the wooden spoon back to the bowl. 'Add more black pepper and salt.'

'I was going to,' I said. Alicja chuckled. I gave her a wan smile.

'Look at your sister.' She poked her index finger into the dough to check its softness. 'Well done.' She lifted Alicja's blond fringe and kissed her on her forehead, leaving a white flour mark on my sister's nose with her thumb.

'Perhaps I should get pregnant and then my cooking skills could improve dramatically,' I snarled, grinding spices in a beech pepper mill.

'Have you fried the onion yet? Of course you haven't. Why am I even asking?' my mother said and started to peel the onion which was lying on the table next to me.

'If you give me a chance,' I said,

'You are too slow.'

'Whatever,' I muttered in English.

'What kind of wife will you make, if you are so slow? And don't "whatever" me.'

'You know what, I have no idea,' I said. 'I guess I will be happy if I can avoid poisoning the unlucky man. I'm sure you will take good care of him.'

'So,' my mother changed the topic, ignoring me, 'We better start thinking about buying a pram for the baby!' She clasped her hands in excitement. Then, humming to herself, she placed a big pot under a stream of cold water and added chopped vegetables and herbs.

'Mum, I think it's a bit too early.' Alicja tried to cool down her enthusiasm. My sister walked to the sink to wash her hands, bits of dough stuck around her fingers. 'The doctors said we should wait and make sure my body will not reject this pregnancy.'

'I don't want to hear silly talk like that. Of course you will give birth to a healthy boy,' my mother said through her teeth. She was holding four safety matches in her mouth while vigorously chopping the onions. The sulphur in the matches neutralized the onion juices and stopped her from crying.

'A boy!' I looked at Alicja. 'She has already decided for you. How nice.' Alicja kicked me under the table.

'I know, Mum. But I don't want you to get your hopes up before we know for certain. That's all,' Alicja said and wiped her hands on a dry kitchen cloth.

'It's different with IVF,' I joined. 'Sometimes the body rejects it.'

Mother looked at me with tears in her eyes. I was not convinced the match trick worked. 'Nobody asked you for an opinion,' she muttered.

'Mum, listen,' Alicja interrupted sensing she was just about to say something which would lead to an uncontrollable exchange between us. 'I'm just saying that we should wait a bit.'

My mother added chopped onion to the pot and lit a fire underneath.

'What are you making?' I asked.

'Carp in jelly.'

'Disgusting.'

'Yes, the whole family knows you can't stand it, so you won't have to eat it,' my mother gave me a pitiful look. 'It is for your father and me. And I am sure Alicja and Krzysiek will have some as well. Now, your sister is expecting a baby and I want her to eat proper food.'

As if jelly was proper food but what did I know about feeding pregnant women?

I knew Alicja detested that dish as much as I did, but my mother insisted on making it every Christmas, and although she did not force us to eat it, we were usually presented with an irresistible slice of it. 'You are not even going to try it?' my mother would say in a fake surprise. If we still refused to touch it, she would deliver one of her famous lines, 'I slaved for a whole day in the kitchen to make it and you do not even want to try a tiny bit?' When we answered that we did not ask her to make it she would get so upset she would start to cry and the only way to make peace with her was to force the bloody fish in jelly down our throats.

My mother busied herself with peeling boiled beetroots. 'Magda?' she pronounced my name with an unusual melody and I began to feel uncomfortable. I sensed what was coming. 'When are you going to get married? You are over thirty already.'

'I am a human traffic accident; no children, no husband and over thirty,' I said.

'I am simply worried about you.'

'Then stop. Marriage and having kids is not the kind of thing I want in my life,' I said. I finished preparing the filling for pierogi, and hoped, this time, she would be satisfied with the seasoning. 'I'm done. Would you like to taste it?'

She put the vegetable knife down and bent over the bowl to try some, using the wooden spoon I used for mixing. 'Add a little bit more salt,' she mumbled with her mouth full. 'Can't you taste it is still a bit bland? When you finish, you can start preparing the meat filling.'

She went back to her table and continued grating the boiled beetroots. 'I don't know why you are so sensitive about it?'

'About what?' I asked.

'Marriage. Kids. It's only natural.'

'Because every single time I come to visit, you always end up talking about the same thing over and over again,' I replied in a tired voice.

'I am your mother.'

'I know and I love you but just let it go, Mum.'

'You are going to be very lonely when you get old. You know that? And children and family are the most important things in life. Look at Alicja, she is finally pregnant, thank God for that,' she raised her eyes to heavens. 'I wish it was earlier. Ah, well, you can't have everything. At least your sister has finally realised what's important in life.'

'That's Alicja not me. And I do not want to have children because I will feel lonely when I am old. Nobody can guarantee that my children will take care of me when I'm old. That's selfish.'

'That's not what Mum meant,' Alicja interjected and shot me a reproachful glance. I could not understand why my sister was taking her side all of a sudden. I searched for an answer in Alicja's eyes but they were impenetrable. Was it the first sign of pregnancy, turning her into somebody I could no longer recognise? The old Alicja would have joined the conversation, dissected the argument on both sides, rationalised the origin of the issue. My aggressive irony had not met with the reaction I expected from my sister.

'I guess you're speaking about yourself because you do not visit me unless you have to. At least I have Alicja.'

'That is not what I meant! Why do you always have to twist what I say?' I stood up and walked out of the kitchen.

'That's it. Walk out! That's what you are best at!' I heard my mother's raised voice behind my back.

'Mum, Magda, can you please stop quarrelling. It's Christmas. Why do you always have to fight with each other?' I heard Alicja, but I was already in the living room trying to find a pack of menthol cigarettes in my handbag. Why did I let her upset me? Didn't I know better? I knew my mother. I knew what she was like. I could not hold it against her that she said those things to me. I decided I would not let her feel that there was something wrong with me.

I found the cigarettes and opened the door into the garden. My fingers were trembling from cold.

'Are you all right?' Krzysiek touched my shoulder, gently squeezing it. He took one of my cigarettes. I handed him the lighter. I bent my head with a cigarette in my mouth.

'The usual,' I said, blowing the smoke through my nose.

'Mother?'

'Yep.' I did not feel like talking, especially to him.

'After Christmas you could come back home with us, to Warsaw. I really would like you to. You know that.' He was playing with my short hair but I brushed his hand away. Through the glass door I saw Alicja entering the corridor but she didn't notice anything.

'Really? Thanks, what a relief. But I think I'll go back to London.'

'You have definitely learnt sarcasm in London,' he said, stepping away from me.

'You think so? Or maybe I simply don't feel like talking right now. Why don't you go and talk to somebody who cares.' I wanted to say, like Alicja, but I stopped myself. It was Alicja who was gripped by a proud feeling of possession over him, not me.

'Fine. I'm going inside,' he said, his face sour, and dropped the cigarette butt on the snow covered grass. 'Are you coming?' he asked with his hand on the door handle.

'I'll be back in a minute. I want to have another one,' I said. As he went inside he made sure not to let Alicja see his dejection.

You see, it was a difficult time for me that Christmas. I questioned myself. Where was my life going? Was I making the right decisions? Would getting married and having children be the best way to sort out my future? I was near defeat. I wondered what it would take for my mother to accept me the way I was. But I already knew the answer. She wanted something I could not give her. She wanted me to submit to her ways. Only then she would be happy. But what about me? What about what I wanted?

I heard the door being opened. It was my father. He held a woollen shawl in his hands which he wrapped around my shoulders.

'Thank you,' I smiled.

'Don't take it personally. You know what she's like,' he said. He was standing next to me holding a glass of the Hennessey

I had bought for him, a Christmas present I decided to give him early.

'Do you like it?'

'Yes,' he handed me the glass and I took a sip.

'Strong,' I licked my lips.

'Listen, Magda, just do whatever makes you happy.'

I thought how different my parents were.

'Has she always been like that? I mean, when you were younger. Was she always so nosy and controlling?'

'You are not so different from each other.'

'In what way?'

'You both fight. You should let it go sometimes. And to answer your question, yes.'

He was starring at the evergreen trees in front of us.

'I really admire your patience.' I looked at his face.

'Comes with age,' he said still looking at the trees.

His voice had a note of bitterness, although he tried to hide it behind his gentle smile. I often wondered how he managed to stay with my mother for so many years, almost thirty, if I remembered correctly. I would not blame him if he wanted to get a divorce. Which I thought he would do after I witnessed him kissing another woman, on the lips. He never kissed my mother like that. Her face looked familiar and then it hit me that she was one of my parents' neighbours. Mrs Kucharska was a widow with no children. Perhaps it was the fact she was nothing like my mother that attracted my father to this woman. At first I thought it was my father's middle life crisis but Mrs Kucharska was my father's age, a soft-spoken, usually dressed in black, hardly a person you would notice if you had met her on the street.

Alicja did not believe me and I was not going to stalk my father and take photos to prove my point. I never mustered the courage to ask him either about the other woman or why he chose to stay with my mother. Perhaps I did not want to know.

He finished his cognac. 'Come inside. It is minus thirteen degrees. I don't want you to catch a cold.'

She was so relieved the first day was behind her.

The Christmas performance began the next day in the steaming kitchen with my mother skilfully holding three different spoons, trying each dish, adding final touches by sprinkling seasoning here and there. The fried carp in white wine sauce had five more minutes in the oven, two types of pierogi, with meat, cheese and potatoes, sizzled on a second pan, and a clear beetroot soup with mushroom ravioli was now ready for serving. I felt out of place when I looked inside and retreated to the dining room to help Alicja lay the table with a white tablecloth and place candles in the middle.

'Magda! Alicja!' we heard. 'Are all the plates ready on the table?'

'Yes, Mum,' Alicja answered, before I had a chance to respond.

I walked around the table, placing cutlery beside each plate and the wine glasses. The cat observed the whole commotion from underneath the table.

'Don't forget to put a plate for a guest,' added my mother, sticking her head in from the kitchen. Her cheeks were flushed from cooking and streaks of hair moist with sweat clung to her ears. She wiped her forehead with the back of her hand.

It was traditional to have an additional plate on the table for an unexpected guest. In case there was a homeless person or somebody knocked on the door, we were supposed to invite them to our table. It never happened, but each Christmas we kept this tradition.

'Look what I bought at the market today.' My mother walked into the dining room holding a small picture wrapped in a clean kitchen cloth. Her hands were wet.

'What is it?' Alicja came closer.

'It's a painting of a Jew with money, for luck.'

'For luck?' I asked.

'Magda, how can you forget all our Polish traditions? A few years abroad, and you don't remember you are a Pole!' My mother unnecessarily raised her voice. 'If you have a Jew with money in your house for Christmas, you will have the money for the whole year,' she explained slowly.

I never recalled this particular tradition. A line of Primo Levi occurred to me: 'We preserved the memories of our previous life...' Why would my mother buy a picture of a Jew? As if she had deliberately erased from her memory the subsequent events of hatred; Oswiecim, Brzezinka, the pogroms in Jedwabne, Kielce, the post-war anti-Jewish violence. How much more had she chosen to ignore? Because it was Christmas and her job was to preserve heritage? What heritage? What an irony of Catholicism and its tradition in Poland. As a child, I was told by priests who visited my parents' house that Jews killed Jesus. Now, my mother was celebrating the Jews as a talisman for good luck, because in our mentality a stereotype of a rich Jew – the Jew banker, the envied successful Jew – represented the status we craved and hated at the same time. For my mother it was an imperative to preserve the tradition, not the reality, which could be ignored in order for tradition to flourish.

'I don't know what to say, Mum. It's wrong. Don't you see what you have done?' I asked, stumbling on the words, because it was my mother.

'You are unbelievable. You know, I seriously begin to think that it is better for us that you have left.' She wanted to add something but Alicja grabbed the picture from her hands and butted in, 'It's really lovely. Where are you going to hang it?' I admired the way Alicja defused the atmosphere. I wondered whether she learnt that while dealing with difficult clients at work.

Mother kept her eyes fixed on mine for a brief moment, with a look I had never seen before, as though she doubted I was her own blood because I dared to contradict her beliefs, which had become alien to me. She turned her face to Alicja. 'I was thinking in the corridor or actually, in the kitchen, here,' she placed the picture on the wooden shelf, next to the window. 'All right, girls, I think we are ready. Call father and Krzysiek to join us,' she instructed us. I noticed her bitter expression when she looked at me.

When we left the dining room, Alicja whispered, 'Can you do me a favour and just pretend you are enjoying yourself. Can you do that?'

'You can't be serious,' I said. 'After what she has said?'

'Oh, please. What difference does it make?'

'I told you I didn't want to come but you didn't listen to me.'

'This is not the time to talk about it.'

And I thought, it never is.

I went to the other room to ask my father and Krzysiek to come to the dining room. They were playing a computer game on my father's computer. When I walked in Krzysiek was about to obliterate a monstrous creature spitting blood on the computer screen. They reluctantly hit pause on the game when I told them dinner was ready.

My mother carefully placed the beetroot soup in a large ivory bowl in the middle of the table, and Alicja and I went to the kitchen to bring the rest of the dishes, twelve according to tradition. While we walked from the kitchen to the dining room carrying bowls, plates and casseroles, my mother went to her bedroom to change her clothes. When she got back she was wearing a navy blue long dress and kitten heel black shoes. The only jewellery she had was a pair of freshwater pearls.

'Where is the Christmas Wafer?' she asked, walking in and tying her hair into a bun.

'It's here.' Alicja handed her a small plate with thin layers of oplatek.

Krzysiek and my father, both dressed in jackets, white shirts and ties, were engrossed in a discussion of the best strategy for how to defeat the monster in the computer game I interrupted.

'Is the first star already shining in the sky?' My mother asked and Krzysiek looked out through the window.

'Not yet. But it's a bit cloudy and it's snowing. Maybe we should start anyway?' he suggested.

'Let's begin. Wesolych Swiat!' My mother wished Merry Christmas collectively to the whole family. Then, she approached each one of us with a plate in her hands with oplatek which we broke and held in our hands. I waited at a distance until my parents, Alicja and Krzysiek finished wishing each other Merry Christmas before I approached my sister.

'My dearest sister,' I said, 'I wish that everything will be fine with the baby and you will soon be a proud mum.' I placed two kisses on her cheeks, then I broke a piece of Christmas wafer that she held in her fingers and placed in my mouth. She broke mine, and did the same.

'Thank you, Magda. And I wish that you find what you are looking for.' I hugged her closely to my body.

I walked to my mother, 'Merry Christmas, Mum. Lots of health and love this year.' I extended my hand with a wafer towards her.

'Thank you,' she said, breaking a piece. 'And I wish that you find a good husband this year and finally manage to keep your job for longer than a few months.'

'Right. Thank you,' I said and approached my father.

He hugged me first so tight he almost squeezed all breath out of my lungs before breaking oplatek with me, 'Be happy and achieve whatever you wish most.'

'Thank you, Dad.' I closed my eyes for a moment while holding on to him. His beard scratched my cheek but I didn't mind.

I looked around, searching for Krzysiek, but he had already moved to the other side of the room where he stood clinging to Alicja's body, like a child who constantly needed reassurance that his mother was within reach; touching Alicja's hair, stroking her cheek, placing his hand across her waist. I stood watching them until she noticed me and gently pushed him away, indicating with her head that I was waiting to wish him Merry Christmas.

'You know,' he began breaking a piece of my wafer, 'I didn't think you would actually come for Christmas. But here you are.'

'Here I am,' I said and waited.

'Merry Christmas,' he said and slowly kissed me on my cheek, breathing lightly into my ear.

'Merry Christmas to you, Krzysiek,' I said quietly. I was feeling tender towards him, but I was afraid to say that I was sorry for what I had said to him yesterday, aware of Alicja looking at us. Perhaps it was Christmas time that made me so momentarily weak, the immediacy of my family that made me feel so lonely at the same time.

We sat down at the table. Ewa Bem's voice, singing Polish carols, played in the background on my father's CD player. Mother placed mushroom ravioli on each soup plate and poured clear beetroot soup over them. The first Christmas dish. Then we helped ourselves to the rest of the food. By the time we finished dinner, I could hardly move.

'Now we can open the presents,' commanded my mother, when Alicja and I had cleared the dirty plates. My father had already started preparing coffee for all of us. 'Krzysiek, why don't you see what's under the Christmas tree.' He kneeled next to the tree and fished out the first packet. He read aloud our names, which were written on the cards attached to each present. My mother received the largest number of presents.

A few hours later, around eleven at night, my mother announced, 'Jakub, Alicja and Krzysiek, Magda, time to go to church.'

The midnight mass – pasterka – was a permanent fixture during Christmas at my parents' house. Strange, but I can't recall the last time I went to church, especially for pasterka. It has the feel of a theatrical performance where the priests are like actors in a Shakespearean drama, with solemnity on their faces, conducting a legion of middle-aged women in singing carols and bending their heads in religious fervour.

'I think I'm going to stay at home,' I said, making myself comfortable on the couch in the living room.

'What do you mean? Are you not coming with us?' asked my mother.

'I said I'm not going.'

'I'm not deaf. I heard you the first time. We are a family and we are going to church. Now, put your coat on.' She spoke in a voice I remembered from childhood. She had a voice that didn't ask but issued commands.

Conveniently, everybody had already left, not to bear witness to an argument between me and my mother.

'Magda, I don't understand,' she said.

'Mum, listen,' I braced myself to say something I should have said a long time ago but I had never had the courage to face my mother. 'I don't believe in God. That's why I don't want to go to church.'

'Oh, is that so? Then why did you come this year?' She folded her arms across her breasts which had lost their elasticity after she gave birth to me and my sister.

'Because I wanted to see you and Dad?'

'If you come here you need to behave like a member of this family.'

'What does going to church have to do with it?'

'This is what we do. We have always done it. You know that.'

'I am not a six year-old child any more. If I don't want to go, then let me stay. Can we just drop the subject, please, mother? I don't want to argue with you. Everybody is waiting for you downstairs.'

'Why can't you be like Alicja?'

'So this is what it is about.'

'You are wasting your life in London. Look at your sister, she has a great job, she got married and now is expecting a baby. What have you done with your life so far? Alicja told me you lost another job.' She exhaled sharply, and I promised myself to remind my sister later to keep her mouth shut. She shouldn't have said anything.

'You knew I wanted to leave Poland.'

'Your family and your home are here. You are a foreigner there and you will always be.'

'And you think, if I stayed here, it would have been better for me?'

'Yes.'

'I don't think so. Do you really want to know why I left?' I asked.

'Please, enlighten me.'

'Because of this.'

'Meaning what, exactly?'

'Because you always want to control me, you always think you know what I want, but I want something different. I always wanted something different. I was choking here for a long time. In this country. Staying here wouldn't change anything. Yes, I have my problems in London and life is not easy, but I don't want to live in Poland. I just don't.'

'So you are saying you will never come back?' I heard how she drew the breath in, anticipating my answer.

'I don't know. I don't want to. My home is in London.'

'No. Your home is here. At least it used to be.'

'Mother, please. Don't you see I want you to be happy for me? I am happy there.'

'You've isolated yourself from everything. From us, this country, your roots.' My mother, her hand already on the door handle, stood waiting for me.

'I'm not my sister,' I said.

You see, the sanctity of family meant submitting to my mother, and I was guilty of betraying my family, and by the same token, betraying my country. She regarded my resistance as a destruction of my self. I was her failure. Her fear was that of a mother who somewhere had made a mistake with her own child. She thought I would grow up, which meant coming back. She questioned whether she had done everything right. She thought she had. But I was evidence that perhaps something went wrong. I had changed into somebody she had not anticipated having to face.

'I am very disappointed in you. I wish ... I wish ...'

'You wish I had never come?' I finished her sentence. 'Is that what you were about to say?' I wondered if I would come for Christmas next year. 'Because I do not belong here anymore, I do not belong to this family. Is that what you want to say?'

'Feed the cat. He's hungry again.'

I stood behind the closed door and listened to her heels clicking as she walked downstairs. I wondered what I was running away from: my country, or my mother? The more she pressured me to stay in Poland, the more reluctant I was to grant her wish. It is not easy to admit that what she felt towards her mother was not love. Standing behind the doors, listening to the fading sound of her mother's feet on the stairs I knew she had lost the ability to love her mother. Her mother's unquestioned authority over her as her daughter repulsed her. The sanctity of her motherly right over her, simply because she gave birth to her and me, was not enough to make her love her. Was it enough for me to love her? She was supposed to love her mother simply because she was her mother, because the tie between us was absolute.

I do not know why this part of my life has made me now so suddenly melancholic. It is difficult for me to recall these memories in front of you, to begin to understand whether I was deliberately cruel, testing my mother's love for me, betraying her and my sister. I sometimes wonder what is worse, what hurts the most: emotional or physical betrayal?

The next day after breakfast I escaped my parents' house. I spent hours walking the streets of my hometown, stopping in front of the windows of restaurants and cafes and observing couples holding each other's hands, families with children, searching for something in their faces. Were they really happy? Were they arguing like I was at my home and now sought a respite in public places, where the arguments begun at home could be politely put aside for later?

My sister called me and told me to wait for her in one of the cafes in the Old Town, on Solny Square.

'I want to go back to London,' I said.

'You can't run away every single time you have an argument with Mum.' She glanced at the waitress's slim waistline and placed her hand across her belly and rubbed it gently. 'Figure out what you want with her.'

'I shouldn't have come for Christmas. I should have known it would be a mistake. I tried to tell you, to avoid the embarrassment.' I was playing with a lighter.

'Don't be stupid.' She took the cigarette from my fingers and inhaled once, and she gave it back to me. Her fingernails were neatly manicured.

'Aren't you supposed to quit?' I asked.

'It was one puff.'

'You better eat a chewing gum before we get back home. By the way, thank you for not telling her I lost another job.'

The waitress brought our coffees and arranged the plates with cakes on a small table between us.

'It must have slipped out,' she said, moving the cigarette packet and a lighter away from the plates.

'Try not to let it slip out next time, okay?'

'You are like a cat and a dog.'

'She loves you more than me.' I crushed half of the cigarette in an ashtray and placed it on the floor, by the table leg.

'That's ridiculous.' Alicja cut a slice of chocolate cake with the fork.

'You know I am right. You have always been the successful one with a brilliant career, a husband and a baby. You are her dream come true. She never lets me forget that.' I added three spoonfuls of sugar to my double espresso. 'I have already changed my flight. I'm leaving tomorrow.'

'We are having the baby to keep us from splitting,' she said slowly, weighing her words carefully. I waited. 'Nothing lasts forever, right?'

'Aren't you happy?'

'Happy, happy. What does it mean anyway? Just a word. Listen, I know mother can be a difficult person to be around. But you've got to admit you aren't an easy person to be with, either. And I know it must be very hard for her to understand why you left. I don't think she ever accepted it. And you haven't exactly made it easy for her, have you? You just took off without discussing your decision with anybody. So I understand when you say you feel tired, but there's also another side to it.'

'Do you still love him?'

'Of course. But love is not enough. You need something to keep people together. You need something to hold on to.'

I knew I needed my sister to hold on to whatever remained of the real me.

It was late afternoon when we got back home. My mother opened the front door and left us in the corridor to undress, and walked back to the kitchen. She didn't have to say anything but we knew she was upset because we had failed to show up on time to have a family lunch. In our family, eating times were sacred.

My mother looked relieved when I informed her about the flight change. It came so easily to her to accept that I was going back to London. Her fake surprise during our conversation was almost unnecessary. She was waiting for me to apologise, which I did not want to do. Why should I? It was not me who had started the whole argument. And it was not only about our argument. I could feel she resented being in my presence. She busied herself in the kitchen, heating up some dishes for me and Alicja.

'Mum, can I talk to you for a minute, please?' I asked.

'What is it? Can't you see I'm a bit busy at the moment?' Her eyes were focused on the sink while she was vigorously peeling the potatoes. The cold water running from the tap made her fingers red.

'About the flight tomorrow. I think it will be better for everybody.'

'You mean it will be better for you.'

'No.'

'If that's what you want to do, then go.'

'Aren't you going to say something?'

'What do you want me to say?' She lifted her gaze. She left both her hands in the sink, holding a potato and a knife. 'If you want to go, go. I'm not going to force you to stay with us.'

'You can't pretend that nothing happened last night.'

She dropped the potato and wiped her hands on her apron, then moved to check on a piece of fish in the frying pan, 'Pass me the salt, please.'

I walked towards her, holding a ceramic container with coarse sea salt.

'Look at me,' I said and grabbed her hand. 'I wish you could understand what I want. I don't want to constantly fight with you. Please.'

'Magda, there is nothing I can do about it. I asked you to go to church and you didn't want to, and you know how important that is. Then you said those awful things to me. So there is nothing more to say.'

'You know it is not about church,' I said irritably. 'I want you to love me the way I am. I don't always know what I am supposed to do, but I am trying really hard to do what's right for me.'

'And you think going back to London tomorrow is the best thing?'

'Yes.'

'Then go. But don't expect me to be happy about it. It's Christmas and you are supposed to be with your family.'

'I know.'

'What is more important to you than your family? You live in London by yourself, alone. A person cannot live on her own all the time. You need to decide what it is that you want.'

'I'm trying but you are not helping me. You want me to be like Alicja and I am not.'

'You were never like Alicja and I've always known that.'

'Sometimes I feel like you love her more than me,' I said quietly.

'That is not true.'

'It feels that way.'

'I am sorry you feel that way but I love you both the same way. Which doesn't mean that I don't have expectations of both of you,' she added quickly. She now took the plates from the cupboard above her head. 'You are my daughters and I want the best for you both. I think you are making a mistake by living there. I think you should come back and make your life here. How much longer do you want to stay abroad? And do what? Change jobs every five months? Pass me that knife.' She placed a chopping board on the table and took a plastic bag of frozen dill and parsley from the freezer.

'What about your insurance and retirement? I know this is the last thing you'll be thinking about but you need to face reality. What you have in London is not a real life! It's a great adventure, I admit, but it is not real life. You think I never wanted to leave when I was your age? You probably never thought about it. But I did. Then I met your father and I thought - you need to appreciate what life's giving you. I could have left, even when I met your father. But I made a decision that it was not worth it. I didn't want to feel like a stranger every day living somewhere where I wasn't wanted. I want you to settle down, have a family, build your life.' She wiped her hands on a kitchen cloth and placed a clean hand on my cheek. Her fingers were freezing cold. 'Life is not about doing everything that you want.'

'I am sorry but I can't. And coming back to Poland is not going to change anything,' I said.

'This will always be your home. Not there, or wherever you want to go,' she waved her hand towards the window before she placed both hands on my shoulders, 'but here, with us.'

'I have a home, Mother, and it's in London. And it is where I want to live.'

'All right.' She turned away and got back to unfolding frozen herbs from the plastic bag to sprinkle on top of the potatoes.

'Mum, I ...' But she did not let me finish.

'You better start packing.'

Strange how telling you all this makes me feel, like a spectator of my own choices, all of which led us to where we are now. At times like now I do not enjoy telling you about those events. It seemed so simple at the beginning. A few days ago, on a plane to see you, I thought endlessly about the events I am describing to you now, trying to find the best way for us to understand each other, or for you to understand me. Perhaps in the end I will fail. Perhaps whatever I say about myself does not matter anymore. It seems like another story, a stranger's story, and you are listening to me only because we are family. Would you listen to me if you knew who I really was, what she and I had done to the people you did not have a chance to learn to love? Would you?

six

NOW, I REALISE I HAVE SPENT the whole morning talking about the family and neglected the most important thing – my next job. By now you should have an idea but there are still some things I would like you to know about. Because if you come with me in a few years, you will need a cover job as well if we want this relationship to work long term.

You should know that most employment agents in London are the same type of scum – the bottom feeders whom nobody actually needs but they are there anyway. The jobs they advertise rarely exist so there is no point trembling with excitement. They place you in the companies that suit them best. To them you are simply a number. And they almost never call back. They do not have to pretend to be nice because the turnover of the candidates always ensures a fresh blood supply. Finding a job in London was not without its challenges. At first I was politely informed that I did not have London experience and, as a result, I was not allowed to apply for permanent jobs. After I acquired London experience I was told I was changing jobs too often. After I stopped changing jobs I was told I was stagnant in my career. Whose fault was it? But adding more fuel to my mother's monotonous complaints about my broken and meaningless life (her words) was not something I wanted to be exposed to during each telephone conversation or my short trips to Poland. My mother is simply too ignorant of the way things work and she could not understand my situation. Now I think she has given up on finding any reason for the kind of life I have in London.

After I returned home after Christmas I spent days looking for something I could do next. I followed online advertisements on *The Guardian* jobs section and *The Times*; I applied for hundreds of jobs, sent my updated CV to my agents and waited. It did not matter what I was doing next or where I was going to work as long as I had some kind of employment.

Finally, fed up with the silence, I called an agent about a part-time job I saw advertised on their website. It was a position in a global finance consultancy but with my poor track record in previous employment she was not convinced I could be successful. 'You have nothing to lose,' I said to her. 'The worst-case scenario is that they don't hire me,' I added to make her feel more comfortable. She was not, but she sent my CV to them anyway.

I checked their website, the usual polished crap: 'passion for excellence ... respect ... diversity ... thinkers anticipating market trends ... team spirit and community involvement ... social responsibility ... creating value.' My head was spinning from all the positive messages. It was all wonderful and exhilarating and meant fuck all. A perfect place for somebody like me.

I memorised all the key words from their website and went for my interview.

Whatever it was, my infamous directness, attitude or persistence, I got the job, much to my agent's surprise and my mother's relief.

Although there were two executives, Jaipal Udayan and Steve Mills, it was Jaipal who became my main responsibility. The second vice-president, Steve Mills, assured me from the start that he did not need me. And after a few weeks on the job I was certain there was no chemistry between us. Steve, with his hearty glottal laugh originating somewhere at the bottom of his throat, or possibly from his slightly overweight stomach, could not hide a certain resentment towards me.

The only thing Steve used me for was to fetch him a soup from Eat; Big Simple or Big Bold of the day. Five years of MA studies and I was a dog for lunch because Steve was too lazy to do it himself. At the beginning I had half mind to leave but at least working with Jaipal required brain power; I could engage with activities other than running around. I did not want to let Steve make me believe there was something wrong with me, or anybody else.

'Now that you work for me,' Jaipal said one morning, 'people will judge me by the way you look and behave.'

'So no drinks tonight with the rest of the staff for me then?' I asked.

'I am saying that you should be careful because they hired me to make unpopular decisions and some people will try to get information from you. I don't want you to get too drunk and then say something you aren't supposed to say.'

I needed this job. I was not going to argue with him.

And so, the longer I worked with Jaipal, the more I became like him. I was quickly given an appropriate nickname – Rottweiler: loyal to my boss; quick and efficient when I needed to grab somebody's balls and drag them to Jaipal's office; ruthless in executing deadlines. In any case, people in the company seemed intimidated by Jaipal and felt a certain unease about me as well. It seemed like I had finally found a niche for myself. With a contagious laugh, Alicja concluded that I had finally set myself free.

I am not a people person: team-building exercises bore me, volunteering for company events is a waste of time. After my disappointments in previous workplaces, I largely avoided colleagues and curbed my inclination to form friendships. And after I came to the conclusion that Alicja

was jealous of the people I became close to, I was careful with
my foreign relationships.

Eight months later I was still working for the same company,
the longest position I had ever managed to hold in London.
That was an achievement on its own which made me extremely
proud of myself, and I dutifully informed my mother about this
unprecedented event. Well done, was the only thing she said,
waiting for the day that I would I lose my job. Wisely, she did
not have high expectations of me.

Then it happened. Human Resources with their Big Brother
attitude, a bunch of overzealous individuals desperate to
pretend they knew what they were doing in managing others,
were never my cup of tea. As far as I am concerned, they are a
redundant category of people, creating unnecessary tension
among staff in any office. Perhaps if they weren't so preoccupied
with poking their intrusive fingers into everything, their
presence would be more palatable.

Cynthia Fisher, the brightest star in the Human Resources
department, was a prime example of a person I could happily
obliterate from my presence if we had met on different ground.
You are probably wondering now what I mean by obliterating
her. I admit it is not an accurate choice of word. In my business
getting rid of people – or, to be precise, having people who
for a certain amount do it for me – happens sooner or later.
It's simple. I must protect the business. Let's say for now
that Cynthia was not dangerous to me. Annoying, yes, but she
did not endanger my business so I did not need to use such
drastic measures.

Besides, it would have been so easy and why waste my
money on somebody like her?

Whenever I bumped into her around the office she beamed,
baring her upper teeth with her mouth slightly open, as if she
just had the orgasm of the century. She spoke in an overly
friendly tone in her high-pitched voice, pretending she was an

innocent little girl and there was nothing to be afraid of. Cynthia was full of positive energy, exploding like an atomic bomb the moment she launched off in pursuit of her unprepared victims.

I had numerous and pointless meetings with Cynthia Fisher about how I was fitting in, whether I was happy. Did I want to change anything; did I want to do something different; was I positive about my life and my career path; was I getting along with the other women; did I have enough work to do; maybe I was overworking myself; was I using my lunch breaks to relax; was I emotionally balanced? Cynthia bombarded me with questions about my wellbeing like a concerned machine gun. It did not matter that I answered all the questions as positively as my depressed soul allowed me to. Cynthia Fisher was a persistent bugger.

'There are new partners joining the company and I would like you to work for them,' she announced one Wednesday in her angelic voice.

'I am not sure I follow,' I gave her a wan smile. 'What about Jaipal and Steve?'

She closed her eyes and smiled, as if I was a child who needed a bit of guidance. 'You see, Magda, this is where you're wrong. I am your boss.'

'You are?' Surely I would remember such a tiny detail from when I was employed eight months ago.

'I assign assistants to different partners. The time has come for you to move on and work for somebody else. It will do you good.'

'It must be a misunderstanding,' I said. 'With all due respect Cynthia, Jaipal is my boss.' I was determined to stand my ground.

'No. You are part of the Human Resources team. You and Jaipal are a good team but you shouldn't assume you are irreplaceable.'

'It would never cross my mind.'

'Oh, Magda,' she gave another condescending smile while her eyes were surprisingly fixed on mine, 'I thought we were friends.'

Sorry to disappoint you sunshine, I thought, but friendship does not register in my vocabulary when I am listening to you.

'You are my friend, right?' she continued. 'This company is like a family and we all support each other.'

Maybe she spent too much time looking at the company's website or maybe it was her who wrote this crap.

'Perhaps I haven't been clear,' she said, looking at her wedding ring, which she was now playing with. 'Your loyalty should be to Human Resources and to me as your boss. You will be working with a number of various partners depending on their needs. But it is ultimately my decision where to place you.'

Which I quickly translated as: 'Don't fuck with me because I can make your life miserable if I want to.'

Like I said, an overzealous, unfulfilled and probably frustrated member of the Human Resources profession.

'There is a partner meeting coming up and I know that Jaipal has assigned you to run it from London. I'd like you to perform as best you can.' She took a sip of tea from her mug, clasped in both hands. 'There is one person I should warn you about and it's important that you fully understand the circumstances. One of the people coming to help you with organising this event is Lotta Lejeune, the chairman's best friend. How to put it,' she hesitated, which was unlike Cynthia. 'Lotta can be a bit blunt with people, and there were some complaints about her, but nothing serious,' she quickly added, 'I assure you. I'm telling you this to give you a heads-up because I know you're a tough person yourself and you might find working with her, well, slightly challenging.' I was almost overwhelmed by her concern.

'Any suggestions?' I said.

'I'm sorry but there's not much you can do.' She swirled the remaining tea in her mug, lifted her gaze and added, 'But

I don't want you to get nervous or anything. You'll be fine. I'm sure you will be great.'

'Isn't it a Human Resources issue you should be able to deal with?'

'We acknowledge it's not an ideal situation.'

'She's the chairman's best friend and that's the end of the story.'

Cynthia remained silent with her impenetrable smile. I took particular pleasure in making her uncomfortable by tossing at her the same corporate bullshit she was throwing at me.

'There's not much we can do. I am sorry. I'm saying this to you now so you can be careful,' she said.

I readied myself to leave.

'There is one more issue I would like to discuss with you before you go. Some concerns have been raised about you.'

'Concerns?' I sat down.

'That you are not smiling and you look tired.'

I said nothing.

'Yes. You tend to look sad when I see you around in the office. And it is not only my observation.'

'I come to the office to work. I don't have time to entertain people around me. Who said that anyway?'

'That is confidential information and I am not allowed to disclose it,' she said, getting serious.

'Anything else?'

'You don't seem to show positive energy when you come to work.'

Was this place some kind of feel-good office therapy? How about we all stop working and start beaming and cracking jokes so that we can have 'positive energy' spinning around and flooding the place with rainbows and pink happy balloons? I heard about people working for Disney who had to dress as Mickey Mouse or Donald Duck but I did not expect to be a cartoon character in a consultancy company.

'Is that also one of the confidential comments?' I asked.

'It is a general comment made by various people.'

Dear, oh dear, I thought, they probably have undercover psychics at work who walk around the desks and check the positive energy levels among the workers.

'You are also perceived as stepping above your position and can be unapproachable,' she finished, at last.

'Any comments from Jaipal?'

'No. He is pleased with your work,' she said reluctantly.

'Good to know there is at least one person who is happy with me,' I muttered.

'Magda, you are a very bright and hardworking young woman. I personally would like you to succeed in the company and I am saying this to you so that you can work on your attitude. Trust me, I am your friend.' She put her hand on mine.

'Can I go back to work now?'

'Right. I'm very happy we have had this conversation and cleared the atmosphere.' She breathed a deep sigh of relief but it was me who should be worried now. 'You can now move on and start afresh. Thank you for your time. I just wanted to make sure that you are feeling positive here with us and to let you know there is room for improvement.'

Now, how was I to explain all this to my mother?

seven

IT WAS A SUNDAY and I was sitting at home, waiting for a phone call from Krzysiek. Alicja was at the hospital in labour. It had been four hours already and I was getting very nervous. I kept texting him but he wasn't responding, and I was worried something was wrong. Finally the phone rang.

'It's a girl!' he exclaimed before I had a chance to ask him anything.

'How's Alicja?'

'She's very tired. She lost a lot of blood. I thought she wouldn't make it,' he said quietly.

'What do you mean? She's okay now, isn't she?'

'Yes, yes, she is,' he assured me. 'Although she is very weak. Magda, the doctors came and asked me who to save first. I didn't know what to do.' His voice was breaking. I had never heard him so vulnerable. I almost believed it.

'You should have called me. She's my twin sister. It's my decision.'

'She is my wife.'

'You don't understand her the way I do,' I said. But what I really wanted to say was that he did not love her the way I did. I was surprised how easily Krzysiek claimed my sister, now that she had given birth to their first child.

'Is my mother there?' I asked.

'She's with Alicja now.'

'Can I talk to her? Can I talk to my mother?'

'Maybe later. I'm sorry.'

'Have you got a name?'

'Marianna.'

'My middle name?'

'Alicja insisted. You're an auntie now. Big responsibility.'

'I know,' I said, trying to conceal the weakness in my voice.

All of a sudden things were getting serious in my life, or was it that life was steadily moving on and I had not noticed? I wanted Alicja to be proud of me, to believe I could handle the responsibilities of having a niece, even if I consider children a nuisance, a waste of space, at least in my life. But having a niece was different. She would not expect twenty-four-hours-a-day-seven-days-a-week attention from me, unlike from her mother. I gorged on my freedom and found it difficult to subscribe to the whole ethos of marriage and procreation. It was a daily nightmare of looking at a child as if it was a different species which had suddenly landed on my planet, invading my existence with a big unknown. I wasn't ready for any permanent attachment, especially one that terrorized me into complete submission. I thought of parenthood as a life sentence and I certainly had no inclination to enter wilfully into a cell where I would be surrounded by toys, milk bottles and nappies, while my brain effectively disintegrated into unrecognizable mush. And by the time the children were big enough to take care of themselves, if that was ever possible, I probably would not remember who I was before. And I would always be perceived as the person I was, afterwards.

You see, I never agonised that there might be something wrong with me, like my mother did. I never doubted my life choices. And I never felt there was something missing in my life. But one noticeable side effect of my decision to remain childless and unmarried is social ostracism, certainly not in London, but among the people I left behind. I am not invited to drinks, house parties, family gatherings. My female married friends, who are often already proud mothers of two or sometimes three, rush their husbands out of my vicinity, as though I have a highly contagious disease. Perhaps the fact that I do not babble incomprehensibly or my face does not melt into bliss when the mothers blatantly exhibit their toddlers in front of me contributes to the substantial decline in the number of invitations when I visit Poland.

And there are rarely any topics that I can safely discuss with the women who have become mothers. They certainly do not want to discuss abortion, women's rights, military conflicts across the world; even a supposedly safe question, like 'What have you read recently?' poses a challenge. 'Promiscuous' was the word I often overheard whispered behind my back, because there is nothing worse than a barren and single woman with time and money on her hands. They certainly think there is something wrong with me because no sane woman chooses to remain childless.

You see, my honest rejection of motherhood was another way in which I became a foreigner in my own country.

I never fully understood Alicja's need to procreate but I accepted it, like she accepted my choices, or at least she tried to. Unlike me, she did not spend time weighing in her mind the disadvantages that came with motherhood.

'It's something you do. You just know,' she once said to me. It was not enough for me. The practicalities of motherly responsibilities or any form of inconveniencies and sudden alterations to your daily routine were not things Alicja considered. Motherhood to Alicja was almost like another highly demanding client, and she was determined to be successful. Whereas I was relieved to be in London, away from the maternity ward.

That night I opened a bottle of champagne and drank it all. I was toasting my freedom and Alicja's child.

On Monday I went to work. The day began with a morning meeting with Jaipal. When we had finished looking at the upcoming meetings, projects, conferences and his travel arrangements for the next month he asked me to stay behind and tell him about the meeting with Cynthia.

'I told you when you started,' he said when I finished, 'I am not popular and this is one of their ways of getting back at me. Just do your job. It's office politics, that's all. And besides, there will be some further changes in the company. The management is looking for a new buyer and you need to prepare yourself in case I'm not here anymore. Maybe it won't be such a bad idea for you to work for somebody else, if you have the time, of course.'

'Let's worry about it when the time comes, shall we?' I was more than aware that with Jaipal gone the likelihood of me losing my job was high. Cynthia would make sure of that.

'You know I hired you to protect me from the crap I don't want to deal with, and maybe to do it with a smile? Can you at least try?'

'I wouldn't expect rainbows shining out of my ears,' I said and got back to my desk.

Baring my teeth whenever I bumped into Cynthia failed to grant me emotional amnesty in her eyes. Every time she passed my desk, she would put two fingers to her lips and stretch them in a wide grin as a signal to show my softer side.

Well, Rottweilers are not particularly famous for wagging their tails, are they?

I blamed my cultural background. I simply was not prepared for the spiritual awakening that Cynthia was prompting in the office because, like it or not, I was an emotional miscreant. I had never so fully and consciously wished that I had been born in the UK. There were times when I wished I had been born to a different mother but that was hardly something I could change as easily as I got a new job, so there was no point thinking about it. I was certain that that moment, when Cynthia pressed her neatly manicured fingers to her lips, forcing my lips to crack in return, was when she decided I would never fit. It was time to get rid of me.

The lesson I have for you this morning is as follows – don't underestimate who you are dealing with. It is better to assume that your opponent is cleverer, has more resources and better contacts, and knows your weak points better than you.

The global partners' meeting was taking place in a five star hotel in Hertfordshire. Lotta Lejuene travelled separately, directly to the hotel. Although I remembered Cynthia's warnings about her, I did not ponder what Lotta was really like. The fact that she was the chairman's best friend should have been enough to trigger a red light in anybody's head.

Bill, an IT manager, accompanied me to provide technical support on site. We arrived forty minutes later than we expected.

'You could have left the office earlier,' Lotta said, and left my hand, which I had extended to greet her, hanging in the air after we entered the room that had been assigned as the back office throughout the three-day summit.

'London traffic,' I said, looking at an anorexic around thirty year-old woman.'Next time, don't be late.'

Bill began to assemble laptops and cables in the far corner of the room, which led out to a vast, meticulously maintained garden with a golf course in the distance. Before I managed to get my head around what I was supposed to do, I experienced a foretaste of Lotta's authoritarian regime. She ordered me to go to my room and change my clothes – they were all wearing jeans while I was still dressed in my office outfit. I had trouble understanding her English, which consisted mainly of imperatives, and I ignored her. Then she grabbed my pay-as-you-go phone and assumed I was going to share my number with the rest of the team. 'You have to be contactable,' she said. I told her to give it back to me and arrange for a company mobile phone as I had no intention of footing the bill for business calls. She wasn't a person used to being contradicted but I stood my ground. She found me a working mobile phone surprisingly quickly. When Lotta began to speak Dutch and continued to do so for the next two hours I went upstairs to my room.

After helping myself to a rum and coke from the minibar, and a small joint for a good measure, I stayed in the room for half an hour before she went back downstairs, relaxed and ready to face her nemesis.

'Is there anything you'd like me to do?' she asked.

'I have more experience than you. I'll take it from here,' Lotta said to her and got back to her conversation in Dutch with a woman sitting next to her.

'Go for it,' she said. 'I'm going for a quick fag,' she said to Bill. She stood up and walked through the door leading to the garden. Bill followed her although he was a non-smoker.

'Cunt,' she said when we were well out of their earshot.

'Smile and nod. Let's do our jobs and we can go home. It's only three days. Can you handle it?' He asked her with concern in his voice. He was afraid she would blow up at some stage and it seemed like an enticing idea to me.

'I fucking hope so,' she said.

The last thing she needed was an anorexic skinny-arse crazy bitch who thought she could boss her around with her ignorant language skills.

And so Cynthia's warning voice suddenly came alive in my head. It finally dawned on me what she meant.

The day seemed like a painful spot on the buttocks that was too agonizing and awkward to squeeze.

That first night, after Jaipal arrived in Hertfordshire with six other partners, we all sat in one of the three bars in the hotel.

I drank as if on the Titanic. It must have been around eleven when Lotta and her faithful admirers walked in. I figured out they didn't feel like networking with me as they installed themselves in the opposite corner of the bar. She gave me one of her we-will-talk-tomorrow looks, but the amount of alcohol in my bloodstream erased her face from my short-term memory, and I happily continued topping up on gin and tonic. Lotta stayed less than an hour and when she stood up to leave, the whole group faithfully followed her.

I got back to my room well after two in the morning with a head hammered by too much alcohol. I decided I wasn't going to lose my sleep over Lotta Lejuene. Come what may, I thought, and sunk into the pillow.

The next day, on Saturday, the alarm clock went off at seven. Lotta Lejuene wanted us to be in the meeting room at eight o'clock sharp. I looked at my watch and decided to indulge myself with five more minutes in bed before the shit of a day hit the fan.

Somebody's banging at my door woke up me. It was Bill. I looked at the watch. It was five to eight! Shit, I thought. I released myself from the duvet to open the door.

'Hey, Bill. Come in. Good morning,' I said, trying to suppress a yawn.

'Nice,' he said eyeing me. 'Do you know what time it is? Lotta will be furious. We really need to get going now.'

'Jesus, man, chill. I know, I know,' I moaned and realised I had a terrible hangover from the last night. I needed a big breakfast to survive this day. 'Give me a moment. Why don't you go and wait in the main room, will you? I won't be long.' I rushed to the bathroom to get myself ready.

'Is this a joint in the ashtray?' he shouted.

'What?' I asked. 'Oh, that. No, of course not. I rolled a cigarette.' I was hoping he would not smell the remains.

Less than twenty minutes later I walked out of the bathroom fully dressed and with make up. 'That was quick,' said Bill. 'I've never seen a woman who could get ready in fifteen minutes.' He laughed.

'Let's go,' I said. I placed the joint in my handbag.

We rushed downstairs to the meeting room, passing the breakfast area on the way. It was already twenty past eight, and although I was craving a big portion of eggs and bacon, I thought it would be better if we showed up as early as possible.

'You are late,' Lotta said the moment we entered.

'Good morning,' Bill and I said at the same time. 'I'm sorry it's my fault. I overslept. Is everything all right?' I asked.

'You are late,' Lotta repeated. Her narrow lips were tight.

Perhaps she had hearing problems. With a pounding headache, her squeaking voice drilled into my brain, coming dangerously close to releasing my other self.

'Is there a crisis or something? Why don't you cut us some slack and let's move on to what we're supposed to do today,' I said.

'You are so rude!' she suddenly shouted at me, her saliva spitting like a cobra's. 'You cannot work properly and you are not a team player. You are late! And you want your breakfast. We here to work, not party. You can't even use a Dutch keyboard layout!' She sat down with her concave chest heaving up and down and reverted to quick Dutch.

Oh dear, I thought, all this intensity before nine in the morning. She could have benefited from smoking my weed and relaxing a bit.

'Lotta, I'm sorry. How many times would you like me to apologise? And we did ask you yesterday to speak in English. How would you feel if I started to speak in Polish?'

'That is not my problem,' she said.

You see, either I was going to kick her arse really bad and lose my job or try to calm down and think reasonably for a minute. To start with I decided on the second option. I asked her to come with me outside, to the garden. She said no but I repeated my request. Once we were outside I offered her a cigarette. She refused, although from her nicotine stained fingers I knew she was a heavy smoker.

'Listen, I'm really, really sorry I was late. I apologised a couple of times and it would be great if you could just let it go.' Although I tried to make myself as clear as possible I had a feeling Lotta had already withdrawn from establishing any form of modus operandi with me. Because she did not say anything I continued, 'I don't appreciate being told off in front of everybody. If you want to have a go at me, be my guest, but do it outside.'

'You deserve it. You are not professional.'

'I can tell you don't like me. Fair enough.' I saw contempt in her eyes. 'We don't have to be friends.'

'Your behaviour yesterday was very bad.'

'What are you talking about?'

'In the bar. You sat with the partners.'

'And?'

'You are not allowed to sit with the partners,' she stated, her face contracted in seriousness.

'For your information I was having a few drinks with the partners and my boss, Jaipal Udayan, who invited me to join them. What was I supposed to do, say no?' I was slowly losing my patience with her. 'Besides, I don't see why I should explain myself to you.'

'I'm going back. We have work to do,' she said. She left me standing in the garden.

Perhaps it was my fault we failed to establish any form of meaningful communication between us? The fact that her language skills were impaired did not help. Her thin lips, a fragile, almost heartbreaking physique, and her irritable nature and squeaking voice made me uncomfortable.

She reminded me of a nun who taught me and my sister religion during our primary school years. Sister Zyta seemed like an extension of God's wrath when she repeatedly smacked the back of children's heads for not memorising prayers. I sometimes thought she had a personal vendetta against me. Or was it because my father was an atheist? She blacklisted me for questioning the miracle of the Immaculate Conception, without sexual intercourse between Mary and God, which almost sent my mother into a nervous breakdown. And when Sister Zyta overheard me calling her a religious fanatic, who consciously rejected science and biology, she asked my parents to withdraw my name immediately from the class. The only consolation that my mother was left with was Alicja. My sister cajoled my mother with her negotiating skills and, as a result, my mother persuaded Sister Zyta to religiously educate at least the other twin. Yes, Sister Zyta and Lotta Lejuene could shake hands.

'That bitch is driving me freaking crazy,' I said to Alicja on the phone.

'It's just two more days and you can go back to London.'

'You don't understand,' I interrupted her. 'She's going to complain about me, and there are already complaints that I am not smiling and don't have positive energy in the morning.'

'Well, what would you like me to say? You aren't a sweet little kitten or a bundle of joy in the mornings,' she chuckled. My sister, on the other hand, was up at four each morning for her daily gym routine, before going to the office. 'But seriously, don't beat yourself up over it. It sounds full of rubbish anyway. She obviously has something against you.'

'I could kick her arse so badly.' And I thought to myself that it would actually require only one phone call to have this situation resolved within the hour.

'And from what you are saying, she probably deserves it, but calm down. It's not going to help you in any way.'

'But it would feel good,' I grinned.

'Worst-case scenario you will just get yourself another job. You need to be a better negotiator.'

Then she told me I should come and see Marianna. I asked her about food at the hospital, whether the nurses were taking good care of her and the baby, and when she was going home. Alicja was still in the hospital when I called her. I felt guilty that when I finally managed to speak to her I talked about my job problems, so meaningless when she had been fighting to stay alive. Not once did I ask her about the birth. I did not want to go back to the events of that night. You are probably asking yourself now what kind of a person am I? Before you form any hasty judgments about me, I want you to know that I was never ready to face the possibility of losing Alicja. What was the point in going through the details of a scenario in which she had died that night? Yes, my behaviour may seem irrational to you, even stupid. Not talking about something does not mean it does not affect our lives. I chose not to ask her, and Alicja, as if understanding my fears better than I did, did not reveal how terrified she had been that night.

I prefer to go back to the story of my cover job. Besides, as I said earlier, I do not see the point of dissecting events which had never happened, even if they were highly possible. Best to focus on what actually took place.

I did not use a mawashi-geri kick or the help of my well-paid thugs on Lotta, though my growing anger could easily lure me into doing something unpredictable, something I would surely regret. Instead I avoided her for the most of the day and, in order to protect myself from the temptation of stepping up to war footing with her, I stayed close to Bill. It wasn't difficult as he too, felt an angry apprehension towards her. And Lotta's stubborn insistence on speaking Dutch made it only easier for us to maintain some distance.

After a few unsatisfactory attempts to befriend her, we decided it was pointless. Lotta clearly wasn't interested in speaking to us. She preferred to glow with pride among the partners who praised her for organising the London summit. If that was how she wanted to play the whole thing, it was her decision, and Bill and I could do nothing about it. To start with, we could not communicate with her when she spoke her mother tongue. And being the chairman's best friend opened all the doors for her, because almost everybody wanted to have Lotta on his or her side and have a good word passed to the chairman by her. Which she did, but only about the people who were nice to her. I was sure I was not in the circle of trust, not even on the horizon. I only hoped I would be insignificant to her. At least then she would not play a wounded drama queen in front of everybody and blame me for her bad mood.

Lotta approached me while I was sitting with Bill in the corridor, waiting for one of the meetings to finish. I pretended not to see her.

'What are you doing?' Lotta barked, stopping in front of us.

Poor Bill looked perplexed. He wasn't used to women like Lotta.

'It's a private conversation,' I said. 'I can be with you in ten minutes when I finish.' My expression was placid.

'The meeting is going to finish any moment now and I want you on standby in case they need anything.'

'I said I'll be with you in a minute,' I said quietly but firmly, but it wasn't me speaking anymore. It was her, waking up inside me.

Just as she was turning back to Bill, Lotta grabbed her hand. Before Lotta had a chance to react she jumped from her chair, twisted Lotta's arm from hers and locked Lotta's bony limb in her fingers.

'Don't you dare touch me, ever,' she hissed. 'If you want to talk to me, then wait until I finish.' Bill, an anguished look on his face, gently touched her other arm but she brushed him off.

'You're hurting me,' Lotta mumbled. She let go of Lotta's arm.

She looked at Lotta, impassioned. 'You are the problem. I tried to talk to you but you don't seem like a bright enough cookie to me to understand what's going on. Do you want me to carry on or is that enough for you?'

'No.'

'I thought so. Unless there is something you want me to do I suggest you back off.'

The door to the main meeting room opened and the partners began to come out for their coffee break.

'Let's go,' she said to Bill.

'Where did you learn that?' Bill asked, looking at her closely, assessing whether she would have hurt Lotta if he did not stop her in time. 'Martial arts class?'

She shrugged.

What was she supposed to tell him? About the karate and kung-fu lessons she had taken since she was a child. It was her father who told her to try some form of physical activity so that she could learn to control herself. Funny to think of it now, but in my business the skills she learnt during the martial arts classes have become a necessary skill.

Jaipal followed us down the corridor.

'Are you okay?' he asked. Bill walked behind us. 'It didn't look good when you grabbed her arm.'

'I have had enough of that stupid bitch. I should have kicked her arse a long time ago. She deserves it. She's been on to me since day one. I don't have to put up with her. If I'm going to lose my job, so be it.'

He was right. What was I thinking? After all, it was not the first or the last time I got myself into such a situation. Why did I even bother?

It was sickening that she could get away with everything and nobody dared to contradict her. However much I longed for my boss to back me up, he wasn't going to jeopardize his standing in front of the chairman over this. The only solution was to find another job. I was beginning to lose my faith in ever finding a place where I could feel safe.

You see, the bottom line is that you are always on our own, regardless of the circumstances.

After the unfortunate incident with Lotta, she avoided me for most of the afternoon. I didn't complain. It was in the evening of the same day that she mustered enough courage to approach me. She cornered me outside my hotel room. Had she been standing there all the time? I thought about Jerome, still sleeping in my bed after the quick sex that we had had, and an ashtray with spliff ends. He had arrived the night before because we needed to discuss the delivery routes around the UK. I smuggled him and the weed into my hotel room. Was she eavesdropping? Could she smell anything on me? The last thing I needed was Lotta reporting Jerome to the hotel management.

'I want to tell you that you're doing a good job,' she began carefully. 'We could organise other events together. If you want to, of course. I also would like to apologise if I offended you.' Lotta tried to smile; it was not a smile.

I, she, was not in the mood for reconciliation. Her minibar was empty, she needed more sex and she craved weed. She had no time for this little drama outside her hotel room. She closed the door behind her and said, 'If you want to be a shark, be a shark. But don't come to me for absolution.'

'I thought we could be friends,' Lotta said, coming closer to her and forcing her to lean against the door. Not a good idea!

'Listen, I don't care any more why you are doing this. But don't start all this bullshit about being friends now. You acted the way you acted, now deal with it. But I'm not the one to give you forgiveness and make you feel better. And if you need a friend, go and look somewhere else.'

What was with all these people trying to be my friends? An epidemic of friendship and love or what? Assuming that everybody who is trying to be nice to you is a genuinely good-hearted person is the biggest mistake you can make; you never know when that person will stab you in the back with a knife, and then twist it in further. After some time you learn how to play the system and it's the only way to survive in this place. Trust me! A healthy and realistic assumption that you will be betrayed by the people you think are your friends, or claim to be your friends, gives you an advantage. No. Friendship finishes when somebody owes you money or when a friend becomes a liability and then you have to get rid of that person quickly and quietly. There is no place for second thoughts here. Trust is not something I take lightly. Not in my life.

From now on I decided to keep a record of things that took place. I did not know what to do with the information, and it did not come in handy in this situation, but every incident was a lesson and a potential weapon which could save me the next time that I found myself in similar circumstances. So far I did not know how to play the system. But I was a quick learner. Although I was unable fully to foresee how events would play out, with every disappointment I was getting more cautious. Alicja said I was finally behaving like an adult, taking matters into my own hands, thinking a few steps ahead. At the same time, I had to admit I was not too clever, unable to control my rebellious nature. And that was what happened when I simply could not resist challenging Lotta. I was caught off guard and that was my lapse of judgment. I should have known better. It would never happen again! Deep inside I knew the whole thing would not just go away on its own. I was only surprised by how efficient Lotta was in reporting back to the London office. I underestimated her.

On Monday morning Cynthia Fischer asked to see me, while Alicja patiently waited for my dismissal.

'I heard the meeting was a success,' she said.

'Most people were pleased,' I replied.

'However, there have been some complaints.' She kept her eyes fixed on mine. I, too, gazed into hers, unemotionally. It was the new Anglicised me. 'It was reported that you were not a team player and a recommendation was made not to involve you in any future big events like this.'

I just loved the way she spoke without indicating the exact person responsible for making such recommendation although I already knew who it was.

'Lotta?' I decided to grab the bull by its horns.

'It's confidential information. Unfortunately I cannot disclose who it was.'

'I would like to make an official complaint about the way she treated me.'

'That won't be necessary. A decision has been made,' Cynthia stated. I was hoping for a smile but none was granted.

'Bill will happily serve as my witness,' I said.

'I did tell you to be careful with Lotta.'

'You told me she had a record of complaints against her, so why don't you do something about it?'

'She's the chairman's best friend. There is not much we can do.'

'It is easier for you to sacrifice me than to bring it to his attention, isn't it? You are digging a grave for yourselves. Sooner or later somebody will take you to the cleaners.'

'Are you threatening us?' She braced herself behind the table.

'Oh, no. I'm just stating a fact.' I was savouring the moment. 'But I guess you already know that.'

Cynthia didn't make a written record of our conversation. Although Bill backed me up, nothing was done; soon I found myself removed from Jaipal's team. A month later it was announced that he was leaving the company; it was a matter of time until I went. I was being given less and less work. It was so bad that I managed to photocopy the whole of *The Tin Drum* by Günter Grass and read it during my working hours. The things you can get away with in the office. There was absolutely nothing for me to do. I dutifully informed Cynthia about the lack of work, and I was told that things would improve. Well, they did not.

It probably didn't help that I could not resist making Cynthia's life slightly troublesome. In the midst of this she got pregnant with twins and she was quickly growing to whale-like proportions. She stopped at my desk once to comment on my latest outfit, as if playing the sisterhood card was supposed to clear the air between us.

'Oh, they're so lovely! Where did you get them from?' she said.

'What are?'

'Your boots. I wish I could wear them but my feet are so swollen. I'll be a mum soon,' she said beaming and circling her right hand on top of her belly.

'Don't worry, pumpkin. When you get rid of your excess weight, you'll be able to wear whatever you want. And maybe you'll able to squeeze into a size ten, like me.'

In return, during one of the visits of her mummy friends, who often brought toddlers with them to the office, Cynthia promptly shovelled a screaming bundle into my arms. I kept it at arms length trying to avoid the baby spit.

Perhaps Cynthia could not tolerate my sour face, which by then lost any form of grin I had managed to acquire, or maybe the complacency about Lotta's special treatment was too much to face when she looked into my eyes and knew that I knew. I was eventually informed that I had been made redundant, after almost a year of work. A few years later I found out Lotta Lejuene still worked for the company. Her friendship with the chairman was blooming, fed by the skeletons of people like me who were sacrificed to silence the stinking truth of Human Resources' inability and unwillingness to tackle the problem.

Cynthia Fisher gave birth to the twins and shortly after she got pregnant again, taking advantage of the company's generous approach towards young mothers.

Now I think it is good to know there are at least two happy people with bundles of positive energy. Although I parted from the company, once a year I still receive invitations to the annual get together for former employees. Priceless! I never go.

You see, I was not cut for the corporate environment in the capacity of an office worker. My talents lie elsewhere.

I save people's lives.

Now is a good time to tell you a little bit about some of my clients, because whenever I lose another job I remind myself that in the big scheme of things a dismissal is irrelevant. Keeping my clients alive, observing their successes, is where I take pleasure and pride. I cannot reveal their real names but let's say you will be surprised by the number of well-known people smoking my weed.

I hope you will have an open mind about it.

I have a list of my special clients, the most faithful ones. I sell them my highest quality marijuana. The rest of the product is distributed on the general market. Those on the special list I supply personally. I do not deal with the mass market. Nobody knows my face or name. It is Jerome's responsibility. But when it comes to the special list I like to be able to see my clients face to face. In a way it is my personal indulgence, being able to be seen for what I am.

How do they contact me? Oh, it is simple. I have known these people for years. I have a number of email addresses and pay-as-you-go mobile phones with SIM cards which I destroy after each communication. They only know I can fix them an amount whenever they need it; it is safer for them not to know the real scale of my business dealings. Nobody needs to know everything about another person. It takes careful planning to remember what I say about myself to every person that I have dealings with but it is the only way to protect myself from an unexpected visit from the police.

Judging by your fidgeting in your chair I had better satisfy your growing curiosity.

Lucy is a forty-five year-old actress, competing with her peers to secure the best roles in West End theatres. She says she can remember her lines better and often smokes in a nearby alley next to the theatre minutes before her performance. Occasionally she smokes another spliff in her dressing room and exhales the smoke through a tiny window. Lucy says she loves the feeling of flowing on to the stage and delivering her lines to the ears of the listeners in the darkness. She can hear them breathe and gasp when she delivers her lines. My weed relaxes her. Although she's been performing for over twenty years, she still gets stage fright and has found weed the best antidote to her anxiety attacks before each performance.

Nada is a top-end prostitute who buys weed to smoke with her clients. She doesn't like being called a prostitute; she is more like a provider of hedonistic pleasures that men struggle to find with their wives or long-term partners. They come to her when they want to experience a dream-like moment and forget about reality. She doesn't need to advertise her services. The men who want her know how to find her.

Martin is a City trader who buys from me at least once a month in big amounts. He smokes in the mornings before he goes to work. He says it gives him the edge to trade without getting too ahead of himself while he deals with millions of pounds each day. He also buys weed for other traders and City workers. I take a percentage of his sales.

And there is a highly acclaimed British writer. You will forgive me if I do not mention his real name. He has been shortlisted for the Booker. He even acknowledged me once in his latest publication which was so touching: 'To a very special guardian angel who breathed life into this book when

I couldn't.' Now you understand why on the first day I told you that my clients call me a guardian angel.

You see, I am very proud to be part of their creative process.

Oh, and one more person, perhaps the most influential among my clients. Let's call him Steve, an undercover policeman.

A few years back Steve made me an offer. He would protect me and warn me about police operations and, in exchange, he wanted a steady supply of Cheese.

'I can't do it myself. I can't grow weed in my house. I'm a policeman for fuck's sake,' he said to me. 'Together we can make it work.'

I spoke to Jerome. I did not want to make a decision like that without his knowledge since he is my distributor in the UK. Finally, we both agreed it was worth a shot. Steve is not the only policeman who gets paid by me. There are others.

It took me some time to trust him but Steve proved himself worthy when he warned me about house raids on a few occasions and I managed to relocate the plants in time. Since then, he has been a faithful client. Steve told me about the police hiring military helicopters which scan various areas of London for thermal images. That's how weed growers get caught. You see, since the number of lights needed to sustain a large quantity of plants is substantial, they pop up on police thermal images, which are the quickest and most efficient way to of identifying suspicious properties.

The other problem Steve helped me with is the spikes of energy, also monitored by the police. Now I have my own diesel generator for my own power supply for the lamps. I hired builders, who I paid well to keep their mouths shut, to install the ventilation system to get rid of the fumes and the smell of weed, which can fill the whole house, as well as my furniture and clothes. A small price to pay.

Let me tell you what Steve said to me once.

'The ignorance of society! That's what I'm talking about. Hemp is one of the most versatile plant products. Imagine the possibilities! You can make houses, fuel, clothes, roads, ships, paper, a lot of stuff, and it can be grown almost anywhere by anybody. And the biggest advantage? Hemp-based products are biodegradable. If weed were made legal it could wipe out a number of industries if taken worldwide!'

All this talk about protecting families and strengthening communities that the British government prides itself on, has little to do with the noble cause of keeping society safe. It's about keeping the right industries safe, which they would not be if cannabis hemp were made legal on an industrial scale. And I will not even go into how some police officers raid houses and then sell the same weed on the black market.

I must say I was impressed when I heard him speak like that. With Steve I have become more philosophical about the whole process.

Most cannabis traffickers are not nice people, well, except me of course. They are mostly interested in making money. But you see, for me cannabis hemp has become more than that. When the time comes, I hope it will be the same for you.

eight

AND SO I LOST ANOTHER COVER JOB. But I had a more pressing problem – a trip to Warsaw to meet Alicja's newborn baby. I had promised her that I would come and I was not going to break my word. My parents and I didn't talk much; I kept them at a safe distance, with occasional phone calls, almost no visits. I figured it was healthier for our relationship to keep them at that safe distance. But Alicja, I would do anything for her. Almost anything.

Wait, somebody's knocking on the door. I can hear voices in the corridor. I have to stop.

It was my mother. She wanted more money for Father Maciej because what I had given her yesterday was not enough. Cheeky! Drug money, that is – they will make it holy by sprinkling some water and reciting Hail Mary's in reverent admiration. The Church doesn't shy away from any donations, even if it's blood money.

Where was I? Ah, yes, the trip to Warsaw. Yet, thinking about what I am about to confess to you today, perhaps if I tell you all this through the eyes of my mirror image it will be easier for both of us. I guess it does not make much difference to you, judging from the confused look on your face, but it will certainly make it easier for me. I will be my own witness.

It will help me to reconcile with myself, to remember the events without unnecessarily judging myself. From now on I want you to interpret past events unclouded by any emotions you might have towards me. Before you object, let it be an exercise for you to try. In my line of business family, close friends, anybody we form emotional attachments to, will eventually come to haunt us. And it always comes down to a decision: who is it going to be, me or them? If you need to survive, if it is a question of choosing between you and anybody else, I am telling you now that if you want to live it will be you. You will probably hate yourself for that, every day of your life, but eventually you will come to terms with the inevitability of your choices. Later, there will be no hesitation. The sooner we start your training the better.

It was Krzysiek who picked her up from Warsaw airport. They did not drive directly back home, though. He seemed tense. His knuckles turned white when he held the steering wheel.

'What is it?' she asked. 'You've been quiet since we left the airport. Is everything all right?'

'Yes. I mean, no.'

'What is it then?'

'Let's go for a drink first,' he said.

He parked the car near the Old Town. They were lucky they found a parking place. It was almost impossible, parking being restricted in all the streets around the Old Town, but as he turned into one of the side streets a woman was reversing her car from a spot. They didn't walk far. He chose a small bar with few people inside.

'Now. Tell me what's going on,' she encouraged him, leaning comfortably in a cushioned chair and lighting a cigarette. She had no reason to be nervous, not yet, at least.

'How's the job?' he asked.

'You didn't take me for a drink to talk about my job.'

'Yes. You always land on your feet, like a cat. I don't know how you do it.' His hands cupped around the wine glass. 'It's about Alicja. She's changed since Marianna's birth,' he said slowly. 'She is so focused on the baby. We've been having problems for some time.'

'You never said anything. Neither did she but I shouldn't be surprised by her silence. I assume it is nothing serious, is it?'

'I'm thinking about leaving her,' he finally managed to say it.

'What?'

'Please, Magda.'

'I thought you were happy now, with the child. I don't understand it,' she said. Throughout this time Alicja hadn't said a word to her. But her sister was the one who kept to herself. Was she afraid of damaging her carefully planned image? That Magda would criticise her? That she would have to face the fact that she was a flawed human being?

Oh, for God's sake. What is it now? I have to stop again.

My mother again. I told her we don't want to be interrupted unless it is an emergency. A death in the family, and she is arguing with me about what to wear for the funeral. Who cares? I told her to wear black and leave me alone with you. Let's get back to the story.

Krzysiek told her that they had stopped having sex.

'Have you talked to her? It's probably temporary,' she said.

'You mean not having sex or me moving out?'

'Both.'

'Yes, I have. But she's so focused on the baby. I spend more time at work because I resent going back home. I have practically moved out. I'm renting a flat. I was going to drop you off at Alicja's tonight.' He looked at her glass which she had hardly touched. 'You're not drinking your wine. Don't you like it?'

'I can't believe you didn't tell me about it.'

'We decided to tell you after your arrival in Warsaw. You've had enough on your plate these past few months without dealing with our problems.'

'You should have told me.'

'I know.'

'What are you going to do now? Are you going to try counselling?' she asked and sipped her wine, observing him. She was curious to witness the disintegration of their relationship and how he went about it, as if she almost waited for the damage to happen. She was yet to find out Alicja's side.

'We did and it didn't improve things. She's so fixated on the baby. Like she's obsessed or something.'

'You were very determined to have a baby.'

'Yes, I mean, I thought I wanted it, but now it's overwhelming.'

'Mother will be devastated. The perfect couple is not so perfect after all,' she chuckled. She could visualize her mother's disappointed face. Divorce did not exist for her mother; marriage was for life.

'She doesn't know. Not yet.'

'When are you planning to tell her?'

'I don't know. It's not a priority at the moment.'

'Maybe it's better that you have moved out. You will both have some time to rethink your problems.'

He nodded his head.

'I am sorry Krzysiu,' she said, fondly using a diminutive form of his name. She had not called him that in a long time. He looked at me, searching for the past in my eyes. 'I wish you had told me.' She placed her hand on his and he gently rubbed her fingers with his.

'Thank you.' He put his hand on her cheek and playfully pulled her short hair. 'Come, I would like to show you my flat first and the photos for an album I've been working on.'

'Is it a new one?'

'Yes. From Ghana.'

'When was that? I don't remember you telling me you were going there.'

'It was a short trip. I needed to get away.'

While they drove to his flat he told her about the people he had met in Ghana, that he could not wait to go back and that sometimes he felt like packing his bags and moving to Africa. He said that life was simpler there, stripped back to basic needs. She said he should move first to eastern Poland and try living in one of the villages there with no running water or sewage system.

Krzysiek parked the car in the underground car park. They left her luggage in the boot and walked into the new building; his flat was on the top floor. The flat was an open plan spacious loft with arched windows, and had a view over the rooftops of the Old Town. She did not ask him how much it cost. But he told her he had made an arrangement with his company, which was paying half of the rent. He took her coat off and put it on the cream leather sofa.

'Nice,' she said looking around. She felt a pang of jealousy that he had managed to establish himself without her sister so seamlessly, almost without effort. And there was no guilt in his eyes.

'I got it for you. I remember how you like arched windows.' He left her standing there and walked out of the room to get a bottle of wine.

When he gave her a glass their fingers touched. He stood behind her while she was admiring the view. It was already getting dark. He drew closer to her. In the past she had felt attracted to him but now he was her sister's husband. He kissed her lightly on the neck, his tongue playing against her skin.

'Why are you doing this?' she asked. Instead of answering he placed his hand on her shoulder, turned her towards him and kissed her on her lips. She had forgotten what he tasted like.

'We shouldn't be doing this,' she said, between intakes of breath.

'Why did you leave?'

'Why do you think?'

'I don't know.'

'Seriously? You married Alicja. Remember?' She pushed him away and sat down on the sofa.

'I shouldn't have.'

'Maybe you shouldn't.'

'You left.'

'And what, you couldn't wait for me?'

'I didn't know you wanted me to.' He seemed surprised.

'Please, don't give me that. You knew I wanted you. Wasn't it obvious? But you proposed to Alicja. Don't give me a sermon now about how much you loved me and how you didn't want me to leave. If you really loved me, you would have come with me.'

'I didn't know.'

'Oh, shut up! You are such an idiot. What do you expect me to do now?'

'I want a divorce.'

This made her laugh. 'Just like that?'

'I'll come to London with you.'

'Then what? What about Alicja and Marianna? It's too late for that. The moment has gone. I can't do this to her. She's my sister.'

'As if that stopped you doing anything in the past.' He sat next to her and took the wineglass from her hands and placed it on the floor, next to his. He started to unbutton her shirt.

'That is not the point.' She did not finish because he was kissing her lips again and this time she let him continue. He unbuttoned his belt, dropped his trousers on the floor, frantically taking off his shoes and socks, while she finished undoing the buttons on her shirt and slithered out of her skirt.

He still had his shirt on when he leaned on top of her, propping himself on his hands, afraid to crush her with his weight, and bit her nipples. She took his hand in hers and, greedily, ate his lips and tongue.

'Slow down,' he said into her mouth.

'You want to have a conversation now?' she said, and pushed him to move down. He sank his teeth into her thighs while she spread them open to let him suck on her.

'Alicja never gets so wet.'

She let herself go with his tongue playing inside her.

After she came she pushed him on the floor and sat on him. He held on to her hips, running his hands up her back and pressing his fingers against the skin of her buttocks. She placed her hand on his throat, just when he was about to climax, and locked his breath into hers.

When they had finished she stood up and collapsed on the sofa. He walked naked across the room and picked up a pack of cigarettes and lit two, one for her, one for himself. They lay naked on the sofa, facing each other. He stroked her feet with his left hand, while he held a cigarette in his right, propping his head on his palm. She pulled her feet away, placing them on the wooden floor. 'We're late,' she said.

Krzysiek pulled her back and kissed her on her neck.

'Stop it,' she said, and brushed his hands off her arms.

'You didn't like it?'

'I did. But we have to go now. Alicja will be worried.' She squashed half of the unfinished cigarette in an ashtray that stood on the floor.

'Do you want to talk about it now or later?'

'Talk about what?' She turned her face to him.

'What just happened?'

'Nothing happened. Get dressed,' she said and gulped the rest of the wine. She stood up and began to put the clothes on. He didn't move.

'Then, what was that?'

'You need a definition?' She picked up a shirt from the floor. 'We fucked. That's all.'

'I thought you loved me. I thought this is what you wanted.'

She leaned and placed a hand on his cheek. She thought about Jerome.

'I did love you. A long time ago,' she said, and withdrew her hand. 'But it's over now. We had sex. That's all.'

'I can't believe you're saying this.' He leaned forward to grab his trousers. He walked towards her and put his hands on her shoulders. 'I love you.'

'Oh, please!' She took a step back to pick up her stocking. 'You don't love me. This is not love. You're simply upset with Alicja because she isn't giving you any attention, and I happened to be here. So there you go. A relief fuck. Call it whatever you want. I don't care.'

'I told you I want a divorce. I don't think I love her anymore.'

'Oh Christ, Krzysiek, shut up.'

'You don't think I'm serious, do you? You think I won't do it?' He looked childish; half dressed, holding his socks and belt in his hands. He waited for her to challenge him. He waited for her approval. It was like his plan to go to Africa, a momentary lapse of reason, devising a plan to cling to something that he thought would add meaning to his life. Starting his life afresh and cutting ties with everything that defined him. But he was not like her. Changing his life was always a theoretical enterprise.

'Don't be so dramatic,' she said. 'You're going to work this through. You can't leave her with a small baby. You should have thought about it earlier, before you invited me to your flat.' She was now fully dressed.

'It's not as though I forced you to do anything,' he said in anger and sat down to put his socks on. 'You wanted it as much as I did. Admit it.' He took the wineglasses in one hand, grabbed the wine bottle in the other and carried them to the kitchen.

'All right. I admit it.' She followed him and stood looking at him while he was rinsing the glasses under hot water. 'I wanted to have sex with you. Does that make you feel better? Is your male ego feeling better now?'

'Why do you care?' he asked, still rinsing the wine glasses.

'Because I don't want you to leave Alicja. I think you are making a big mistake and you're going to hurt her more than you imagine. She loves you more than anything.'

'Hypocrite!' He placed the glasses in the dishwasher.

'You shouldn't have had sex with me if you care so much for your sister.'

'Let's say it was for old times' sake, and I felt sorry for you. I did love you once but you married my sister. And it's too late for us.'

She was standing in the corridor with a handbag in her hand, waiting for him to put his coat on. She didn't care about his feelings. Whatever she felt for him in the past, she had killed it. There was no point. Did she feel satisfied that, after all these years, he was now offering to come back to her? Mentally she was in the best shape of her life. She didn't need anybody. She didn't need him anymore.

'Magda, please,' he pleaded, brushing a streak of hair from her forehead to kiss her there. 'We can still make this work. You and me. We deserve a second chance.' He placed both of his hands on her face.

'No, Krzysiek. We will never happen again.'

I can't believe it. It must be my mother again. She's been getting on my nerves all morning. At breakfast she kept asking me what we were doing all day, sitting in this room. I told her, 'Wasn't it your idea?' I said I was telling you fairy tales. She did not believe me. Let me see what she wants this time.

She would like to take you for a walk. I told her to let me finish this story and then she can spend some time with you. She is sitting downstairs in the kitchen. I will be as quick as possible. Besides, I need to make some phone calls, check my email. I know Jerome is taking good care of the garden while I'm here but I like to keep an eye on things.

I hate being interrupted, especially now, when I am trying to tell you about this part of my life, which put us on a course that I failed to see then.

When we arrived at Alicja's house, it was past midnight. Krzysiek placed my luggage in the guest room. When I thanked him he shot me a short glance, which I could not quite place: on the one hand it said that he felt guilty; on the other it said that he condemned me for what we did. My feelings towards him were suddenly confused. I wanted to say that I understood whatever it was that he was struggling with but he was on his own. Alicja stood in the doorway, saying nothing. He quickly brushed his lips against Alicja's cheek and left the house.

'I was expecting you four hours ago,' she said when we heard him closing the front door.

I wished that I had taken a shower at Krzysiek's flat. Could my sister smell him on me? Could Alicja tell that there was something different in his behaviour?

'I'm sorry. We went to his apartment. I know I should have called you. I thought you would be busy with Marianna. How is she anyway? Can I see her?' I kept my voice steady, leaning over the luggage and taking my clothes out.

'Yes. But be quiet. She is sleeping.' Alicja waited until I had placed the clothes in the drawers and then led me into the baby's room.

'She looks like you,' I whispered, looking at the baby.

'She's got your character. She screams and shouts. All the time.' Alicja moved behind me. 'I suppose you've spoken to Krzysiek? Did he tell you?'

I nodded, still watching the baby.

'I'm exhausted. Let's go back to the kitchen,' Alicja said.

'That's why I don't want to have kids.'

'Maybe for once you are the clever one,' Alicja smiled with a flicker of sadness in her eyes. Her hair looked unwashed. The front of her top was stained with some liquid. It must have been her milk. 'Look at me. I mean, don't get me wrong, I love being a mum. It's so different from what I've been doing so far, but it's nothing like in the books. My nipples hurt from expressing milk, I can't remember when I last slept for more than three hours, I haven't had sex for ages and I can't stand looking at myself in the mirror.'

'When is Krzysiek coming back?' I asked.

'This isn't the way I imagined it.'

'Have you thought about hiring a nanny so you can have some time for each other, to sort things out? Look at yourself, you look awful. And I don't mean you being tired. Where's the wonder woman?'

Alicja started to laugh and clapped her hands on her firm buttocks, which were now covered in a layer of fat.

'I know. At least you're not going to tell me I'm skinny! I'm so happy you came,' she said.

'I understand you're embracing motherhood but it isn't the end of the world. It's not who you really are.'

'This is who I choose to be.'

'Really?' I looked around the room littered with packets of unopened New Baby Pampers, used wipes, and baby toys under the glass table. There were dried brownish drops of some liquid on the surface. A yellow rubber duck with a red hat was propped against the legal volumes on the bookshelf. 'I know you wanted to have a baby for such a long time. But are you surprised Krzysiek moved out? I mean, seriously?'

'Are you saying it's my fault?' Alicja pointed the index fingers of both hands to her chest.

'It takes two. I'm not trying to put the blame on anybody. But you let him do it.'

'So now you are saying that if he had left before I got pregnant, that would justify it? That would be acceptable?'

'Christ, Alicja. Shuffling blame from one person to another isn't going to change the reality. You were always the strong one, the ambitious one, and now you have transformed into some warm baby's spit.'

Alicja waived her hands helplessly. She bent down to pick up the toys from under the table. I had never seen my sister like this, so vulnerable, so lost. I hadn't been prepared for that.

'You realise you'll lose him if you don't pull yourself together?'

'Is that what he said to you?' Alicja's voice was momentarily sharp.

I didn't want to tell her that he was thinking about a divorce. Or going to Africa. It was better for Alicja not to know if she wanted to save her marriage.

'What then?' Alicja asked, standing up to place the toys in a basket. She stepped on a blue duck, which made a squeaking noise. Alicja froze and listened in case the baby had woken up.

'I am simply saying,' I continued slowly, 'that being a mum must be a wonderful thing, but there's more to life than that. Let's go for dinner tomorrow. And you both should definitely have some sex. It'll make you feel better.'

That night I could not fall asleep. I heard Alicja walking around the house, back and forth to Marianna's room. The baby cried throughout the night. Despite what had happened between me and Krzysiek, I wanted them to work things out. I was worried about them. Selfishly, I was afraid of losing their marriage from my life. Knowing that Alicja and Krzysiek were together balanced the unpredictability of my own existence. But there was more to it than that. I did not really care about him, but I did for my sister. And he was part of Alicja's life plan. My sister was not made to live on her own. I did not want Alicja to start questioning whether what she did made sense. Having a baby was a natural step in Alicja's life. I was happy for her. Back then, I did not understand why motherhood played such a defining role in Alicja's life, but I understood that it was an expected and natural development.

You see, I did not want my sister to sink into the same dilemma I had recognised in myself. I could not bear to live under the commands of society or my family, who believed in traditions of this land. Perhaps I was too harsh for telling Alicja to get a grip on her life. Her life had always been a perfectly executed existence, even if my mother failed to offer her the freedom to stray from the pre-established order of things. I had managed to run away, but could she? What would become of her if she turned her life upside down? If she chose the path that I had?

With my eyes open, staring into the darkness of the room, the events of the past few years played in my head like a black and white movie, silent except for the accompaniment of the baby's crying. I got up, opened the window and lit a spliff. There was no wind and when I blew the smoke out it lingered for a while in the opening. Who was I? A stranger in my own country. One of Alicja's friends said I did not belong here anymore. You are not from here, I was told. There was something different about me, something they couldn't put their finger on, but something they wanted to press and squeeze, so that the truth about who I really was would burst out in their faces. So they could finally make sense of me. Who cared who I was? They sure care even less now. Perhaps they fear me more than anything.

I had become a chameleon, displaying a combination of accents and faces, depending on what suited me. I was too British for the Poles, and too Polish for the British. I loathed my connection with my home country when I was in London, camouflaging myself on the streets, pretending I did not speak my mother tongue, looking the other way when I heard Polish being spoken. And here, in my own country, I was stripped of my birthright, I was a cheat who left for an easier life. Every wrongly accented word, every sentence which sounded too English, was proof that I was not Polish enough, that I had forgotten who I was, that I had discarded, too easily, my Polish identity. And in London, I was almost a native speaker, but not quite. I could never be too English. But who are you? Who are you really, they kept asking me, here and there. I was whoever they wanted me to be, a kaleidoscopic image with multiple colour combinations, a creature who was accustomed to the environment, until my own self adapted so that I was not there anymore. I flicked the roach through the window onto the street. The baby stopped crying and I went to bed. It was four in the morning.

I slept until eleven. I was still in bed when I called Jerome to make sure everything was in order with the plants at home. When I entered the kitchen to make myself a cup of strong black coffee, Alicja told me she had already spoken to Krzysiek and the three of us were meeting that evening for dinner. I was impressed by how efficient she was. I didn't ask about him because I simply had no time. My mind was elsewhere. I was running late for a meeting with the lawyer that I had scheduled before I arrived in Warsaw. I could not allow the family situation to jeopardise my business. Bribes, arranging the transport of the product out of the country, and laundering the money after the deal was finalised were all I could think of that morning. Usually Alicja would accompany me everywhere, but with a small baby she decided to stay at home. I had never thought about it but her pregnancy was a convenient development. Besides, I did not want her to know who I was meeting. A long time ago I made the decision that I would keep that part of my life away from her.

I got back late in the afternoon. Alicja was in the middle of her preparations to go out. I could hear the babysitter's singing coming out from the baby's room. Alicja had spent three hours grooming her hair and nails, and carefully applying golden shimmer dry oil to her shoulders, forearms and neck. Just before we left, she sprayed more perfume into her hair. She bared her teeth in the mirror to check there were no bits of her late lunch hiding in between them. Then she went back to the bathroom and brushed her teeth and tongue again. I breathed a sigh of relief. She still wanted to work things through.

Alicja's head jerked whenever a new guest came through the restaurant's door. She sat erect in her chair, every few minutes smoothing her straightened hair with her hands, checking that the folds of her dress were where they were supposed to be. Everything had to be perfect, except Krzysiek who was running late.

'He's doing it deliberately,' she said, unable to hide the impatience in her voice.

We had been waiting more than thirty minutes. She frequently stole glances at her wristwatch. Her hands were playing with the earrings that Krzysiek had given her when he returned from Ghana.

'Oh, stop it,' I said, looking through the menu. 'He's probably running late because of work.' I did not know what to expect from this meeting. I only hoped Krzysiek would not betray his feelings, or whatever was left of them.

A moment later he entered the restaurant and rushed to our table.

'I am sorry.' He leaned across the table and kissed her on the cheek. 'You look really nice,' he said to Alicja but she ignored him.

'You could have sent a text message or called. It's not that I have all the time in the world with Marianna. We've been sitting here for more than thirty minutes!' He briefly looked at his Blackberry and placed it in a side pocket of his jacket.

'I said I'm sorry. Do you want to have an argument now or shall we try to have a nice evening instead? It's your choice.'

He took out a pack of Marlboro Red and a lighter, and placed them on the table.

'Oh, don't give me that. You know exactly what I'm talking about,' she said, folding her arms. The lines around her lips rippled when she clenched her teeth, the edges of her mouth twisting downwards when she pressed her lips tightly together.

'Shall we order another bottle of wine?' I suggested, looking at the wine list. The bottle of wine Alicja and I had ordered was almost empty now.

'Whatever you want,' he said and looked around the restaurant to attract the attention of one of the waitresses. I ordered a bottle of Chilean Merlot. Krzysiek was avoiding my eyes.

'What's wrong with you?' I asked him when Alicja left to use the toilet.

'I don't know what you're talking about?'

'You haven't looked at me once. She'll know something's wrong.'

'Hey, it's not me who's pissed off here.' He raised his arms in defence.

'Never mind,' I said and drank some wine. 'Just be nice to her.'

'Oh, for God's sake, I am nice. Did you see how she treated me? Drama queen,' he said. 'I even complimented her. And what does she say? She starts with one of her moods, again.' He opened the packet of cigarettes and lit one.

'Just try, okay?'

'So,' Alicja resumed, sitting down, 'now that Krzysiek has magnanimously granted us his presence, we can finally talk about what's happening in your life, Magda.'

'See, this is what I'm talking about,' he said, stretching his arm and pointing at Alicja.

'What? What did I say?' she asked turning her head from Krzysiek to me.

'Nothing,' I said and fixed my eyes on him.

'You haven't told us how your work is in London,' Krzysiek said.

I was still looking at the menu, turning the pages, thinking about the conversation with the lawyer I had had that day. With the turnover that I was beginning to make, he said that I would have to stop pretending with my silly jobs in London. That was the word he used: silly. I told him that I would make the decision, not him, when I was ready to end this masquerade of office legitimacy. I wondered if I should start looking for somebody else to represent my business in Poland and how much it would cost me to get rid of the lawyer. Still, I needed a lawyer and grooming a new one would take time I did not have. Getting rid of people had become too easy a solution.

'I'm looking for another job,' I said finally.

'Who did you piss off this time?' Krzysiek asked with an amused look on his face. I didn't like it. I wished he would wipe the smirk off his face.

'They told me I didn't smile enough and that I didn't bring any positive energy into the office.'

'I think I'm going to have a salad,' Alicja said and put the menu down on the table. 'Sounds like typical you.'

'I guess I pissed off this woman who was really driving me nuts, but I didn't realise she was going to make such a big deal of it. And then my boss left, and I guess, I wasn't needed anymore. That's it really, without going into details.' I closed the menu. 'Don't you want pasta? I heard they make really good lasagne here.'

'No, I need to lose weight,' Alicja sighed.

'I'll have lasagne,' Krzysiek said.

'Me too.' I joined him.

'You seem to have a natural talent for getting yourself sacked,' Krzysiek said.

'How are the Poles out there?' Alicja asked.

'It depends on the situation. I walk down the road and hear two guys commenting on my arse, and not in a good way, if you know what I mean. I usually turn and say, "Watch your mouth. Some people do speak Polish here." It's very annoying as Poles think the language is so difficult – it's like Chinese is to us – that the odds are you are not going to bump into a Polish speaker. The other day I went to Southampton, which apparently has the biggest Polish community in the UK, to visit a friend. I was standing on the street holding a map in my hand when a woman with a terrified look in her eyes came up to me and said, "Centre? Centre?" I answered her in English, but half way through I realised she was Polish. Her accent was really strong. I switched to Polish and she seemed so relieved. I mean, what are the odds of bumping into a Pole on the street in Southampton? That was before I read that they had almost invaded the place.' I laughed bitterly. 'Then she flooded me with questions about the directions. She wasn't even listening to me when I said I wasn't from there, and had no idea myself where I was. As if it's my responsibility to help a fellow countryman in need. I directed her to one of the Polish shops on the street. The problem with our countrymen is that the minute you start speaking to them in Polish, they treat you as if we were supposed to be one big family, just because we all live and work in the same place.'

'You aren't really helpful, are you?' Krzysiek said.

'Let's just say that I am not a great fan of my own nation. Would you be friends with somebody you don't know on a street in Warsaw? No. But over there, just because we are abroad, all Poles think that we should stick together. Like a big fucking happy family.'

'You are all immigrants out there. What do you expect?' Alicja said.

'On top of that,' I continued, 'they immediately ask you to get them a job and if I don't want to talk to them they get upset.'

'We read in the press about Poles working as fruit pickers, in meat factories, as waiters, cleaners in the hotels. It's not an easy life.' Krzysiek said.

'That's just another stereotype. True, but a stereotype. I think the main problem is the majority don't want to integrate. And those who do...'

'Don't want to have anything to do with the rest, like you,' he finished my sentence.

'They simply want to stay among Poles – Polish food, Polish friends, Polish shops and all that,' I said. 'Most of them don't speak fluent English. Even if I wanted to help them with getting a job, with no language, I'm sorry, but they are not going to be able to work in an office.' I drank some more wine. 'It's fun to reminiscence about the past together, Polish actors, the Soviets, childhood cartoons, you know Bolek and Lolek, Koziolek Matolek, Reksio, but most Poles stay among Poles, and don't make friends outside their circle. It's about the mentality. I can understand that it's comforting to be among your own people, but at the same time it limits any new opportunities. Ultimately, most Poles in the UK live lives of consciously cultivated conformity. And why bother if the majority of them want to go back anyway?'

'And you think that's superficial?' Alicja asked.

'There is this guy – I can't remember who told me this story – who makes barely minimum wage. He works as a washer in a restaurant. He earns so little, he only buys milk and potatoes. He calculates to the penny how much he needs to spend on food each month. As for the rest, he goes back to Poland and spends it on Ukrainian and Russian prostitutes because it's cheaper back home. He comes over to Poland and pretends he's a big shot because he lives and works in London, but nobody realises how poor he really is. So yes, I think it is very pretentious to live like that.'

'People do the best they can. If it keeps them happy then so be it. Not everybody needs to integrate, like you do,' Krzysiek said. There was a note of bitterness in his voice, and I wondered if he was jealous that I was integrating too much with other men in London. He had no idea what my life was back in London.

'It's a choice. But you cannot change your life if you don't try. And staying among Poles, speaking Polish all day long, makes you lazy. No wonder most Poles work as builders, fruit and vegetable pickers, cleaners, factory workers. You don't need a certificate in advanced English to do those jobs.'

'Don't you want to come back?' Krzysiek asked.

'Everybody keeps asking me this question.'

'And?' Alicja looked at me closely.

'I think the times have changed,' I said carefully, hearing Alicja's short intake of breath. 'I'm glad I have the choice to live where I want.'

'As long as you are happy there,' said Alicja and glanced at her watch. 'We better go back. It's getting late. The babysitter will be upset, if we are late.'

'Are you coming back home with us?' I asked Krzysiek. 'All night we have only been talking about me.'

'It is not that simple,' said Krzysiek.

'It is simple. We got married, had a kid, and you have responsibilities,' Alicja said. The waiter came and we asked for the bill. After Krzysiek paid, I stood up and went towards the cloakroom while they remained at the table.

'I didn't realise it would be like that,' he said when I was out of earshot, but I could still hear their loud voices.

'Like what? Like what, tell me!' She attacked him.

'It's like, you only want me to bring in the money. We stopped doing things together, going out, having drinks with friends, travelling to other countries. All these things we used to do before the baby came. Do you remember how much fun we had?'

'You haven't the faintest intention of coming back, have you?'

'I haven't decided, yet. I need time to think.'

'What do you need time to think about? About how you don't love me anymore? Just say it.'

'Of course I love you. It was never about loving or not loving you.'

'Have you slept with somebody else? Is that what it is about?'

'Of course not!'

'You have. I know you have!'

'Whatever I say is never going to be good enough for you, is it?'

'You bastard. Who is she?'

'Alicja, calm down. I haven't slept with anybody. And keep your voice down, please.'

'Oh, so now you really care what other people will think? I hate you. I hate you for leaving me and Marianna. Because we became so inconvenient?'

'Listen, let's talk about it at home, please.' He was trying desperately to pacify her. 'Not here, okay?'

She did not want Krzysiek to come back home with us. We stood in silence outside the restaurant. Krzysiek hailed a taxi, said goodbye and waited until we got inside. When the car drove off I turned my head to look at him but he was already walking in the opposite direction.

'I know he slept with somebody. I just know it. I can smell it,' she said when we finally arrived home. Marianna was fast asleep, thank God.

'Could you forgive him if he did? I am not saying he did, but could you?' I asked.

'No. I don't know. Prick,' she said.

I was trying to decide whether I should tell her. Would she be able to forgive me? I was not ready to take that chance. I could not bear the distrust between us that my honesty would foster, the accusatory monologues, the unanswered phone calls. Yes, I must say I was a coward with my own sister. Now,

I wish I had done things differently with her. I wish I had said something. I should have.

It is time for you to take a walk with my mother. I've kept you long enough and I can only imagine my mother fidgeting in her chair, glancing every few minutes at her wristwatch. I wouldn't be surprised if she was wearing her coat already. I'll let her know you are ready.

How was the walk? Did you enjoy it? Judging from your smiling face and rosy cheeks you had a good time together. Let me wipe the bits of food from your chin. Now, much better, don't you think?

We can finally move on with my story. I hope there will be no more interruptions.

On Sunday morning I left my sister's house as quietly as possible. I left her a note attached to the fridge door, saying that I would be back in the early afternoon.

I arrived at Piotrek's house at nine. He had three cars ready, each with sixty kilograms of weed grown in the container.

'There is a problem,' he said after we discussed the details of crossing the border. The lawyer had already given bribes to the custom officers and I had instructed Piotrek which border crossing to use. You see, everybody has a price. The trick is to find how much you are prepared to pay. Weigh the risk against the profit. People who choose to cooperate with me are well paid. And those who don't, well, most custom officers, most policemen have families, people who depend on them; sooner or later they weigh their own risks. Is it profitable for them to have the people they love injured?

'I noticed root rot,' Piotrek said.

'Are you sure that's what it is?'

'Yes, I'm certain. Black spots on the roots. I'm going to use hydrogen peroxide but I can't guarantee we'll recover them.' He took out a camera and showed me the close-up photos of the affected plants.

'How many?'

'Half. I will inoculate the new ones with predator fungus.'

'Crap. First disease. I knew it would happen sooner or later so perhaps it's better we haven't lost all of them.'

'We'll have to rely on the open air garden. Let me show you something.' He took the camera off my hands and fast-forwarded to the next set of photos of ten-foot cannabis plants. 'Look at the flowers.' The buds were the size of a fist.

'Now, those are some serious buds we have there.' I could barely hide my excitement, my head spinning from the calculation of the potential profits. 'When do you think you'll start cutting them down?'

'In a few weeks.'

'Okay. I am going to get everything ready in London. Listen, I have to go now and deal with some family issues. I will contact you via email when I get back with the details for the drop-off point.'

'Can you get a Polish person this time? I don't like that black bloke.'

'Jerome? You don't need to like him. Get the cars to London and he will take care of the rest.'

Back at Alicja's home, she told me she wanted me to call my mother. I refused. It would end up with another irreconcilable, angry, pointless exchange between us. If I told her I was at Alicja's she would never forgive me that I hadn't taken enough time to visit her as well. It was time for me to go back to London.

It was good to stay for a few days in the country of my birth, but after a while, the nationalistic rampage that I witnessed in the papers and on the television was becoming too tiring for me. I yearned for London's diversity, the different skin colours, faces and languages. I longed for anonymity. You see, our country is predominantly white and homogenous. Anything other than white, Catholic and heterosexual is duly noted and commented on. Even in Warsaw, the capital, there is a limit to human variety.

Racism. Another reason why you might want to consider leaving this place. You are still too young to have a partner, but if you do stay here I suggest you stick to white when the time comes. I don't know how to tell you this but you were born in a backward country. It is sad, I know, but there is no other way to put it.

Believe me, I did my best to understand, to tolerate the names shouted behind my back when Jerome and I flew to Krakow. 'Monkey' was the word they used. I gave up on trying to find tolerance in my heart when we were attacked by a loud group of patriots, from a Polish white power movement, screaming slogans after us, 'Poland for Poles', 'White race', 'Go back to your jungle'. They called me a 'black bitch' for good measure. The police stood and watched as we hastened our steps to reach the rented car and seek protection behind the walls of our hotel room. At least there we encountered only curious glances and whispers when we waited for the lift to take us to our floor.

How can I love this country? How can I ever come back?

Perhaps I should have hired a limo and forced Jerome to wear diamond encrusted neck chains, blasted rap music and let my fellow countrymen enjoy the spectacle. This is the only image they know in this sad land.

But what do you expect from a country when the most feared and powerful priest, Tadeusz Rydzyk, during a mass held for hundreds of people, upon seeing a black priest, exclaimed, 'Oh my God, look at him, he didn't wash himself!' What a great sense of humour!

I don't know whether to cry or laugh when I hear about Polish children at schools in Britain who refuse to sit next to non-white pupils. Did you know that there was a campaign in Polish churches to prepare people for the cultural and racial diversity when they arrive in the UK?

I am telling you, one day, when the Pope is black, Poles will stop believing in God. I wonder whether anybody will dare say that he did not wash himself.

You see, Alicja refused to talk to me about this. I tried, believe me I did. She did not want to get drawn into an uncomfortable conversation in which I would expect her to take a stand. The responsibilities that came with motherhood were as much as Alicja could manage. Did I blame her? Of course I did. I told her that Poland is fast becoming a fundamentalist Catholic state. 'Do you really want your daughter to grow up in a country like this?' I asked, while I sifted through a stack of magazines and papers.

'You think I don't think about it?' she said, running between the kitchen and Marianna's room with a bottle of warm milk. 'I know what you think of me. I know you despise me for refusing to get involved.'

'I don't despise you,' I said, and cut a thick slice of wholemeal bread. I had not had time for breakfast yet and my stomach was rumbling.

'You do. But I have a life to live, if you haven't noticed.' She was now packing used nappies into a big rubbish bag.

'You and your comfortable life. You don't have reasons to engage.' I opened the fridge. 'Is this cheese still edible?' I asked, bringing half a packet of Limburger cheese to my nose.

'Yes.'

'Are you sure?'

'It's fine.'

'If you say so. Smells kind of funny, though,' I said, still holding the packet in my hand.

'It's cheese so it smells funny. And close the fridge, please.'

I smeared the slice of bread with butter and placed slices of Limburger on top.

'What does it have to do with anything? Oh, crap,' she said in anger. The bag split open and the nappies fell on the kitchen floor.

'Need any help?'

'Don't bother. I can manage.'

'Fine. You said your status doesn't affect your judgment. It does. You live in a bubble. All of you. Rich Polish women live in a bubble. You bugger off to Switzerland to have IVF, you pay to have abortions outside Poland, you pay for contraceptives. You can easily afford all this, but what about the rest of the women in Poland?'

'Why do I have to feel guilty about it? You left the country,' she said, her hands under the running water from the tap in the kitchen sink. She splashed some bleach to remove the smell.

'So now you're saying I can't voice my opinion here because I don't live here any more?'

'That is exactly what I'm saying.'

I took a bite of my sandwich. 'Sometimes it's easier to see things when you are not too close to them,' I swallowed. 'Yes, I am really happy I don't live here any more. But you're wrong. I do have a right to say it, because maybe if it wasn't so bad I would have never left in the first place.'

'What do you suggest? That I drop everything and start a campaign against the Catholic Church?' She lifted the rubbish bag with all the nappies and placed it on the floor in the corridor.

'No. That is not what I'm saying. You almost never stand up for me when our mother has a go at me because I've expressed my anger with the Church. And last Christmas you simply obeyed her. Since you got pregnant, you have changed. Like Krzysiek said. As if what we had doesn't matter anymore.'

'Oh, shut up, Magda. Don't even think about bringing what Krzysiek said into this conversation. I don't know what you want from me. My marriage is falling apart, I have to feed Marianna, I have to go back to work at some stage. I can't deal with all this at the moment, and especially your personal vendetta against society, which by the way is your home country in case you've forgotten.'

Alicja disappeared into Marianna's room and I switched on the television. I had five hours before my flight back to London.

'Listen!' I shouted and turned the volume up. 'Somebody has stolen the sign "Arbeit macht frei" in Oswiecim.'

'Are you serious?' she asked, and walked back to the room, holding baby clothes in her hand. 'What do you mean somebody has stolen the sign? How could they have done it?'

'I have no idea. It's made of cast-iron.'

'It was probably some Nazi-loving skinheads or for a private collection. But that's just sick,' she said sitting down next to me. She took the remote from my hands and turned up the volume. We watched the TV screen, which now showed the concentration camp gate and a group of policemen standing next to it, taking photos.

'I don't even know how to judge an action that's so far beyond understanding,' I said. 'If there is no respect, even for the memory of the people who lost their lives in the concentration camps, then I don't know where the fuck this country is going,'

Alicja shook hear head and walked back to the kitchen to load the washing machine with the baby's clothes.

'Let's see how long it will take the police to find the sign. Whoever stole it, they've probably cut it into pieces. How do you punish someone for such an act?'

'I hope that they find who did it very soon,' she said, bending over a box with washing powder.

'Beyond embarrassing.'

'Krzysiek's arrived to take you to the airport,' she said looking out through the kitchen window. 'Are you going to be all right? You know, with your job.'

'Don't worry about me,' I said. 'It's just a job. I'll get a new one. It is not the end of the world.'

'You should go and see mother. I'm serious.'

'Perhaps.'

'You need to talk things through.'

I interrupted her, 'There is nothing to talk about. I'll text you when I land. Let me know how things go with Krzysiek.

Promise me you'll let me know what you want to do.' I held her in my arms for a moment but Marianna started to cry and she turned away.

'I will. Go, now.'

Krzysiek didn't come up and I had to take the luggage downstairs myself. Or perhaps he was not ready to face Alicja.

Instead of greeting me he asked, 'Would you like me to come to London?'

'I really don't feel like having this conversation with you right now.'

'I thought we could spend some time together,' he said, gently rubbing my knee but I pushed his hand away. I didn't want Alicja to see us from the window. I didn't have to look up. I knew she would be standing there rocking the baby in her arms.

'You need to spend time saving your marriage, not coming to have sex with me in London. Let's go. I don't want to be late.'

When Krzysiek stopped in front of the main entrance to the airport, he left the engine running and got out of the car to take my bag from the boot. He seemed to be avoiding me, busying himself with my luggage. Maybe he felt wounded that I had not jumped at the idea of him coming to London. I did not care what he felt. I wasn't going to play the concerned female over his wounded ego. The sex with him was as much as I could handle, but not emotions. Why should I feel responsible or sorry for him? We were both adults. He should have thought about the consequences before he decided to invite me to his flat. I smoked another cigarette and Krzysiek got into the car. He lied that he had to go back to the office. It was Sunday and it was unlikely that he would be working. I watched his car as he drove away. I could see his eyes in the rear-view mirror looking at me. I dropped half the unfinished cigarette on the pavement and went through the sliding airport doors.

nine

GOOD MORNING SUNSHINE! Today I am going to take you for a walk. The car is already waiting downstairs and we are going to drive to the botanical gardens. I thought we could both benefit from some fresh air. Besides, I know I shouldn't be smoking around you. Alicja would never forgive me if she saw me doing this, even if I always open the window in this room. Are you ready?

Now, that bench over there, in the shade of the willow tree, right by the pond looks good to me. Look over there. Do you see the fountain? It's early in the morning so nobody will bother us. It made me laugh that the woman in the ticket office thought I was your mother. I don't know where she got that idea from. Are you comfortable? I brought some juice with us in case you get thirsty. I am dying for a joint. You don't mind, do you? We are in the open air so don't worry. Nobody will smell it.

Look over there. Can you see the top of the tree? It is older than you and me, it's even older than my mother and father. When you are and I are dead it will still be here. Or perhaps one day you can come here on your own and remember this moment. The oldest oak tree in Poland is called Bartek, and it's twelve hundred years old, although apparently this one is only around six hundred and fifty years old. Still, quite impressive.

We will walk over there later and I'll help you find the largest leaves so you can place them between the pages of a book. When I was a small girl I had pages and pages of books filled with leaves from different trees. Now the books are all in the basement. But the leaves are still there.

The sun. Can you feel its warmth on your face? It reminds me of a conversation I had when I dropped off some weed with one of my clients in the City. The weather was exactly like it is today, a blue sky with no clouds.

I was standing by the riverbank, looking at the waves and nearby Tower Bridge and the passing boats. Before my cigarette began to burn my fingers, I flicked the butt into the murky water below.

'You look more bored than I do,' I heard from a groomed and elegantly dressed City trader on my right. I had noticed him circling around me for a while before he gathered the courage to address me.

'I'm not in the greatest mood,' I answered without looking at him.

'If you could have one wish, what would it be?' Oh, I thought, a philosophical conversation during lunchtime. Could be interesting. I answered, 'I would like to be able to fly.'

He guffawed. 'Like a pilot?'

'Like a bird. Just fly away wherever and whenever I want.'

'Sounds like you're having a shitty day at the office.'

'Yep.' We listened to the river waves in silence. 'What would you wish?' I asked him in return.

'Take off.'

'Ah,' I sighed. 'Freedom! The one thing we cannot have.'

I lit another cigarette and watched the tourist ferries. 'Well, enjoy the rest of your day.'

'You're going to be rich one day,' he called after me.

This made me laugh. I was already in the process of becoming a wealthy woman.

Now, time to go back to my story. You are not too hot? If you are, let me know please. The shade should give us shelter from the sun but if you are feeling uncomfortable just let me know.

I decided to visit my parents. On the way home from the airport my mother informed me excitedly of the latest news. She could not stop talking about Alicja and her baby, turning her head to see my reaction. I asked her to keep her eyes on the road.

My schedule was tight; I had appointments with the dentist and the hairdresser, and I wanted to go shopping for hair dye, cigarettes and some clothes. I also wanted to visit a few galleries on Jatki Street, close to the Old Town, and buy some bronze sculptures. A few years back I had begun to invest my money in local art. When you come to my house in London I will show you what I have. My favourite is a girl with pony tails and ribbons blown by the wind holding a bird in the palm of her hand. It is by an artist who died young. A shame, really. I always wanted to buy more of his work.

Late on Saturday afternoon, my mother and I sat in the Soul Café on Solny Square where Alicja and I had had our conversation during Christmas. Soul Café with its mouth-watering raspberry tarts, heavy chocolate cakes, cheesecakes and freshly brewed coffee from a chunky old-fashioned Italian coffee machine is heaven to me. If there is one place I always visit it is Soul Café with its windows overlooking Solny Square, half of it covered with flower stands full of lilies, sunflowers, freesias, gladioli, irises, dahlias and roses in all colours, regardless of the season. There is a round fountain in the middle, which attracts teenagers pumped with hormones, and couples for whom the surrounding flowers offer a perfect place to express their love. I like observing young people, lost in the moment, ignorant in their innocence of the future, imagining what their lives are like.

The customers who frequent Soul Café are mostly the nouveau riche; women in their early thirties with impeccable make-up and hair, sometimes wearing small hats, tall and skinny, clutching Burberry handbags and wearing Manolo Blahnik or Christian Louboutin shoes. Most are either lawyers or own businesses: sports centres, real estate offices, restaurants. Their husbands pop in occasionally, making endless phone calls on two or three mobile phones while their girlfriends, wives, lovers sip coffee in the smoke of thin menthol cigarettes. In between one phone call and another, one sip of coffee and another, the customers cast long glances at the newcomers and passers by.

My mother rarely went out and never to places like that, a celebrity hole, as she said. Sitting and watching people through the window while drinking double espresso has never been her idea of how to spend her free time, calling Soul Café or similar places hedonist caves for people who don't know what to do with their lives. I, too, fell into that category since I frequented similar establishments.

'Marianna is growing really fast. I went to see Alicja last weekend and I'm telling you that girl is twice as big since I last saw her,' she said. 'Alicja has hired two babysitters, although I did tell her that there was no need for that. I can come over anytime and stay with her and take care of my grandchild. Oh, this looks really good. What is it?' She was looking at the display of fruit tarts.

'Maybe she doesn't want you around. With two nannies, that's enough help,' I butted into her streaming sentences and pointed the waitress to what we wanted.

'Family is always better than a stranger. You never know these days. Besides, what I do not understand is why Alicja keeps hiring Ukrainians, Lithuanians and Estonians. The child has to be exposed to Polish not Russian, or God knows what other languages these women speak. If anything, she should learn French and German.'

'When's Alicja going back to work?' I asked, sitting down at a round wooden table by the wall, opposite the main counter.

'That's another thing. I keep telling her that motherhood should take priority over anything else now.' Here she gave me one of her looks to indicate that I was less of a woman for not being married with three children already. 'She isn't young any more and it was her final chance to get pregnant. Thank God she did.' She put her hand on her breasts and tapped herself gently.

'My job is going well,' I lied.

'Good news, I suppose,' she smirked. 'How long do you think you'll be capable of keeping it this time?'

'Oh, I don't know.'

'I am sure they are very polite people. The British are very well behaved. Be respectful and polite and they'll be nice to you, too,' she berated me.

Shall we take a walk now? Stretch our legs? I'd like to show you the greenhouse where they grow cacti from all around the world. Oh, look, there's an ice cream shop. What flavour would you like? Chocolate for my friend, and raspberry for me. Thank you. Let's sit down on the bench over there and eat first before we enter the greenhouse. Can you see the fish coming to the surface on that small pond in front of us? Look over there, on the leaf, a bluetail damselfly. Let me hold your ice cream so that you can have a closer look. Don't run! You don't want to scare her. I'm glad you like it here. Here's a tissue for you. Wipe your hands and sit down next to me.

Where was I? Yes, a visit to my parents.

I found it pointless explain myself to my mother. Without her having lived my life, it was almost impossible to seek empathy from her. When I recalled past events even to myself, they seemed absurd to me now. You see, my mother's world has become like a different planet to me, and mine is even worse; it is a different universe to her.

'You're just being difficult, as always,' she said. 'Look at your sister. She is successful with a baby; she has achieved something, and you? You must admit there is something not right, you know, changing jobs so often.'

'It's not my fault.' I tried to defend myself.

'You've got some serious problems, my child. And I'm afraid to say it but it may be too late for you to deal with them, if you don't start acting like an adult.'

Yes, adulthood, I thought, when did that happen?

'I need to zee de problem eyeball to eyeball,' I said in English, faking a French accent.

'What? You know I don't speak English. Speak to me so that I can understand.' Ah well, the joke was lost on my mother.

'Nothing. Never mind.'

'Typical.'

The waitress brought our coffees and fruit tarts.

'I would like you to start thinking seriously about your future. You can't go on like this,' she said.

'Like what?'

'What about your insurance, your pension? I know you aren't thinking about it right now, but you're not going to be young forever. You aren't a spring chicken anymore.'

'Thanks, Mum,' I said. 'Times have changed. It's different from when you were young and the state provided you with a job for life. How long did you work for your place before you retired?'

'Twenty years,' she answered, sitting up straight and proud.

'Nobody has a job like that anymore. Nobody keeps the same job for twenty years, unless you are, I don't know, an actor or a musician. But even then, it's almost impossible.'

'If you stayed in Poland, you would have such a job by now.'

Yes, Poland was the solution to all my problems, according to my mother, who takes an uncritical view of her own country. How could I blame her? After all she is a staunch patriot, who has never missed a single election since she became eligible to vote, who has given back to society with her two daughters, and who diligently attends mass every Sunday.

'I don't think so,' I said. 'And besides, I don't want to be stuck in the same place for twenty years. Like you were.'

'Still, I have a good pension and no mortgage. And what have you got? Nothing!'

'You were born here and you will die here. I don't want this for me. I don't want the kind of life you've had.' She looked upset, not because my words were harsh but because she couldn't understand that I did not want the life she had. She had the best life she could possibly imagine. Because there was no other. My mother never wanted anything else apart from a steady job and a good pension afterwards. And children, of course.

'You're too young to understand it now,' she said, 'but you will regret it one day. Trust me. You cannot go on like this. And sooner or later, you will come back here, and then you will be old and lonely.'

'I am not lonely.'

'I am not saying you are, but you will be.'

'I like being single and I don't want to get married. Why would I willingly put myself in prison and lose my sanity along the way?'

'You are a woman. You should get married and have children. It's your responsibility. It's what every woman wants.' It was almost unimaginable for my mother to have a daughter who would not get married. Her biggest fear was the inquiring neighbours' eyes when they observed me leaving my parents' house, their faces glued to their windows, because she knew she would have to answer to them and she did not have the answers she was expected to provide.

'You haven't met the right man,' she continued. 'Trust me. When the right man comes, you will want to have children. It's natural.'

'What if my partner was black, or Indian, or from the Middle East?'

'Well,' she hesitated, imagining the reaction in the neighbourhood. 'You can't have children with a person like that, you know that.'

'Why not? What if he was the right man for me? What would you do then?' I knew I was pushing her too far but I couldn't resist it. 'I meet different people, from different cultures, backgrounds, of different skin colour. None of them are white or Catholic, some are Muslim or non-believers, others don't care about religion, not like you do.'

'Magda, if this is what you want, then I can't fight you. But you are Polish, this is your culture, this is your home. Just because you live abroad, it doesn't change where you are from and who you are.' She dabbed her face with a napkin. She took out a small mirror from her handbag and carefully reapplied the lipstick that she had eaten with her tart.

'I've changed,' I said. It felt strange lying to her.

She pressed her point further. 'You will always be a Pole, no matter what, and if you decide to get married to somebody from a completely different culture, of a different skin colour, you will always be different from each other. You won't share the memories that you would have with a man from here. You will always be a foreigner living abroad, and here you will be one of us. Besides, I would like you to get married in church.'

'Somehow I don't think that's going to happen.' She was looking at me, waiting for my explanation. 'I want to officially sign out of the Church. What's it called? Apostasy. That's the name.' I had finally mastered the courage to bring the subject to the table.

'I don't understand what you're talking about.' Her eyes were blinking rapidly, her forehead furrowed.

I put the fork down and continued, 'Please don't get upset. It has nothing to do with you. I simply don't believe in God.'

'Since when?' she exclaimed and looked around, surprised at her own outburst. She did not like drawing attention to herself, especially in public places.

'Remember Sister Zyta? Well, I think that's when it all started.'

'That was the most embarrassing situation you've ever put me in. How could I forget it?'

'Anyway,' I continued, unwilling to dissect the past, 'I have written this letter to the church where I was christened.' I took out a sheet of paper from my handbag and handed it to her. She put her glasses on. 'I need the signatures of two witnesses, to confirm that I'm sound of mind to do it. Regardless of how ridiculous it sounds, I am an adult and can make decisions like this on my own. Still, I guess, the only way the Catholic Church can understand why somebody would commit the sin of apostasy is to explain it in terms of madness.'

'Clearly you are not an adult,' she said abruptly. 'Obviously there is something wrong with you! How could you even think of doing something like that? I am not going to sign it.' She threw the letter on the table without reading it to the end. 'I will never allow it. Never!' She attacked the remains of her raspberry tart with a fork. 'Think about your future! You will not be able to get married in church.'

'I thought we had established that me getting married is not going to happen.'

'What about your funeral? How will your body be buried?'

'I want to be cremated, with no priests crying over my soul. I'm serious.'

'This is wrong. This is very, very wrong.' She kept shaking her head. 'It's excommunication! You have gone completely mad.'

'You know, you don't have to sign it, if it's such a problem for you. I can ask Alicja and Krzysiek to do it for me. I wanted you to know and I was hoping that you would understand.'

'Well, I don't and I don't want to. Do you realize what you are doing? Do you realize what our neighbours will say? And what about Father Maciej? He's always asking about you and he would be extremely upset if he found out about it. How can I show my face in our church?'

'Your local priest is the least of my worries. And who cares about the neighbours? Why are you so upset about all this? It's my decision. This is what I want and I'm asking you to stand by me.'

'I am not going to do it. Nor will your father.' She folded her arms as though to defend herself against my words.

'Actually, I've already spoken to him and he said he would do it for me. He said he would sign the letter.'

'What is wrong with you? You've gone completely mad. It's London. I knew it. I don't know what has come over you, Magda. I don't recognise you anymore. And you used to be such a sweet child. This is not the way we brought you up. How can you be my daughter?'

Yes, that's what my mother said: 'How can you be my daughter?'

Now, we have finished our ice cream. We can go to the greenhouse. Have you ever seen cacti blooming? No? It's a rare sight. Wait, I would like to ask somebody to take a photo of us. Okay, we can go inside.

ten

'WE'RE IN THE BOTANICAL GARDENS. I don't know when. I didn't kidnap her. Please don't shout at me. Mum, calm down. She's fine. I gave her an ice cream. She's enjoying herself. Of course I didn't let her out of my sight. I left the money on the table in the living room, in an envelope.'

Negative. She asked me to take the photo of them together. She can remember my face now.

'Don't touch them. We can buy potted ones on the way back if you want. Come, let's go outside and find a nice spot in the sun.'

She is about to leave the greenhouse. Do you want me to proceed? There's nobody around us. The foliage obstructs the visibility of the cameras in the greenhouse. If you want me to do it now it's the perfect moment. Okay. Understood. Yes, I have enough photos of both of them.

eleven

THIS IS WHAT I SAID to my mother when she said to me, 'How can you be my daughter?'

'I've never felt myself in this country, you know that. I don't want to be a member of the Catholic Church anymore. I don't want to be part of an organisation that covers up child sex abuse by its clerics, which prefers that people should get AIDS and die instead of letting them use condoms to protect themselves, which is against abortion even if a woman is raped. But that's just part of the problem. I simply don't believe in God, I don't think God exists, and I don't see the point in being considered a Catholic. I don't see the point in being a part of an organization which has a long history of covering up abuse throughout the centuries. Open your eyes, mother! Look at what's happening around you. You cannot keep ignoring the reality. How much more suffering does the Catholic Church need to inflict on others? How many more cases of abuse do they need to cover up for you to wake up and realize that this organisation is rotten to the core?'

Mother sat silently, swirling the coffee in her cup. Then she lifted her head and said, 'This is not the way we raised you.'

'What does that have to do with anything? You always put the Catholic Church on a pedestal, refusing to face the facts. How can you listen to them? The Church has no right to dictate to women in this country how to live their lives, influence the law, take away their right to decide if and when they want to have children.'

'Not everybody is bad. There are good people, too.'

'There's a substantial difference because the priests profess to have some kind of God-given power. They believe they hold the highest moral authority to tell us, the ordinary people, what is right and wrong. If you claim a position of moral authority, then, I'm sorry, but you need to reflect it in your own actions before you tell others what to do. How can you follow the Pope who prefers a culture of covering up abuse to transparency? Paedophiles go to prison but not if you are a paedophile priest. They simply run to the Vatican to cover up their shit and live happily ever after, and the victims are sworn to secrecy. It's madness!'

'You are twisting things. And you shouldn't talk about the Holy Father in such a way,' she stated quietly. Her fingers were trembling. It was too late for me to stop.

'Really? Because perhaps your Holy Father would not seem so holy after all if you cared to open your eyes and see how John Paul II dismissed and hushed up and denied the accusations of child sexual abuse by the priests, in Mexico, Ireland, or the US. Father Marcial Maciel, the founder of the Legion of Christ, to give you the most prominent example, was a close associate of John Paul II who knowingly chose to ignore Father Maciel abusing children. And the current Pope ordered Father Maciel to spend the rest of his days in prayer and penance. Or shall I say that the current Pope, true to his name, allowed blessed Father Maciel to spend his last days peacefully, rather than pay for his crimes of sexual abuse. But I guess you wouldn't read about that in your local paper, would you?'

'Stop it. Just stop it,' she said in a whisper.

'You know sometimes I think the Church would prefer people to go back to the Middle Ages,' I said. 'The fact that we're educated and can read and think has been the biggest curse for the Church.'

'I don't want to listen to this any more,' she said and put the coffee cup on its saucer.

'You know, Mother, the sad truth is that the Church exists and thrives thanks to people like you who prefer to close their eyes rather than face the truth. It's all good as long as nobody dares to open their mouth.'

'I want to go home.' She stood up, her face turned towards the window.

'I guess you're not going to sign the letter for me?'

My mother said nothing.

The only hope I had lay in Alicja's ability to convince my mother simply to accept it. My mother waited outside while I asked for the bill. I waited for the waitress and handed her the money. She gave an embarrassed look. I noticed that people in the café had stopped talking. I finished my coffee standing.

We walked to the car in silence. I told my mother that I would arrive at her house later that day because I wanted to do a bit of shopping before I left the next day. I stood on the pavement, waiting until she was out of sight. What I had said to my mother was heresy. She would not call her friends to seek advice on what had been said. It was too embarrassing for her. She would keep it quiet. The doubt that I so eagerly wanted to plant in her would be buried under the habit of her faith. You see, in my mother's case, the ritual of faith is unquestionable, an impenetrable wall of self-protection against anybody who challenges her understanding of God. There is no life without religion. She is religion. Standing there and watching her drive away I knew she thought of herself as the righteous one, the chosen one, the only one who did the right thing. It did not matter what I said. The only thought that had crept into her mind was the question of whether her own daughter had suddenly become the enemy. On that day she decided to protect the family against me at all costs.

Wait a moment. What's this guy doing? Wasn't he the man who took the photo of us together in the greenhouse? Yes, that's him. Strange. Thankfully the park is crowded with families. Do you think we are being followed? Perhaps I am paranoid. Or maybe not. I'll keep an eye on him. If I see him near us again we will have to leave. But for now, let me go back to what I was saying. Where was I?

I did not get back home until later that evening. The house was quiet except for the television with the news on, playing in the background.

'We would like to talk to you,' my mother said when I walked in. 'Come and sit with us.' She installed herself on the sofa. My father was sitting on a kitchen stool. He was still reading the newspaper but he folded it in haste after my mother loudly cleared her throat in his direction.

'Your father and I have decided we are not going to sign the letter.' She sat erect, with the cat on her knee looking, baffled, at our angry faces.

'You've already agreed to sign it. I only need one more signature. Are you backing out now?' I said, standing.

'Your mother is right. Maybe you should think about the consequences. Don't make any rushed decisions.'

'You can't be serious. Why did you change your mind?'

'We both came to the conclusion that you will be making a big mistake by sending this letter. I've also spoken to Alicja and Krzysiek and asked them not to sign it,' she said.

'Why did you do that?' I asked.

'Because she is your sister and she loves you and agrees with us that you are making a big mistake,' said my mother.

'I don't believe you!' I exclaimed. 'Alicja would never do such a thing.'

I walked out of the room to get my coat.

'Are you leaving?' I heard her voice while putting my coat on.

'What does it look like I'm doing?' I shouted back at her.

My father followed me but my mother remained seated on the sofa with the remote control in her hand. She was flicking through one channel after another. My father stood next to me awkwardly, trying to help me put my scarf around my neck.

'Don't be upset, please,' he whispered.

'How could you do that, Daddy? You agreed to sign it. Why?' I asked holding back the tears of anger that were gathering under my eyelids. 'I thought you would understand.'

'I understand but when your mother came back this afternoon, after you had spoken, she was so shaken by this. I didn't realize she would take it like that. I couldn't bear it.'

'So you basically sided with her to spare her tears.' I tied the scarf around my neck and was buttoning my coat. 'She always does it.' I turned my face from the mirror to look at him. 'Terrorizing the whole family with her tears. And for the sake of peace everybody falls for it. Was she crying over the phone as well when she was talking to Alicja?'

'Yes, she was. But that's not the point. You know your mother. But I didn't side with her. She gets very emotional about things. I just thought it would be better that way.'

'It isn't. And she made a mistake calling Alicja. She shouldn't have asked her to do it.'

'I'm sorry you feel that way. I really am.'

'Never mind, Dad. I'll get somebody else to sign it for me. But I wanted it to be you and Mother, as it is a big decision. I didn't want you to find out from somebody else. I had hoped that you would both be supportive. I guess I was wrong.'

'What time is your flight?'

'Nine in the morning. I've already booked a taxi.'

'Don't go without saying goodbye.' He gently pushed me towards the living room.

The unspoken need to keep up the pretence of a happy family, exhibited in our behaviour, was stronger than any argument.

'Goodbye, Mother,' I said standing at the entrance to the living room. I wanted to see her making an effort but she did not move. She just kept switching over the channel. I turned and left their house and went back to my hotel.

That man again. We should be going. I will let the driver know we are leaving. Have you got your leaf? Good. I have to tell you about one more conversation that took place that day. It won't take long. I can tell you it while we walk back to the car.

On Sunday afternoon, a few hours after I got back from Heathrow Airport, I telephoned Alicja.

'Just got back from Wroclaw,' I said, walking around the house with clothes in my hands; I felt they all needed washing after the trip.

'Why didn't you say you were going?' Her voice was calm.

'I don't know. I'm sorry. I needed to see our parents and talk things through. You know what it's like. Anyway, there is something I need to talk to you about.'

'I know. I also need to talk to you about something.'

'You do? Okay. How's Marianna?'

'Good.'

'Krzysiek?'

Silence.

'Is everything all right between you?' I asked.

'You fucked him.'

Now I was quiet.

'Listen, it's not like that,' I hesitated.

'Like what?' She interrupted me. 'You fucked him. My own sister!'

'It just happened.'

'Oh, shut up, Magda! You can have anybody you want but you had to go after him. My husband.'

'How did you find out? He told you?'

'What difference does it make?'

'I guess it doesn't.'

'Why did you do it?' Alicja's voice was frighteningly calm.

'I don't know.'

'I don't want to talk to you. Don't call me back.' She hung up.

I dialled her number again but she did not answer and it went to voicemail. I tried calling Krzysiek's mobile phone but there was no answer, either. I sat down, holding the phone on my knees.

You must be hungry. Let me open the car door for you. What's that you're saying? You want me to buy you a cactus? Okay, wait for me in the car.

What a day! I hope you enjoyed our outing but I think it will be safer if we stay indoors from now on. Before I let you sleep tonight, I still have something more to tell you. A bedtime story. Are you comfortable in your bed? Let me lie down next to you. You can close your eyes if you want and listen to my voice.

I kept checking my mobile phone throughout the day. Finally, I received a very short email from Alicja.

Please don't contact me. Or Krzysiek. I need time. It's best if we don't talk to each other for a while. Don't call Mum.

I did as instructed. What else could I do? I was banished from their life, from my family. I steeled myself not to talk to them, not to ask for forgiveness. I didn't see the point. Do I regret, now, what happened then? No. Days of silence turned to weeks.

You are probably wondering how I managed to keep myself from contacting them. I did not. I wrote emails that I deleted without sending, the same with text messages. Those first few days, I spent hours constructing messages in my head. I never sent them. Then, slowly, I began to erase my family from my mind. I focused on what was around me.

Sixty kilograms of cannabis grown in the underground container made it safely to London. Jerome was distributing it among the dealers in UK cities. Among the faithful ground workers, money changed hands every day. The demand on the streets was growing. I needed to produce much more. If I wasn't going to do it someone else would. I had my own list of clients who were waiting for their supply, but I wanted them to wait for the outdoor plants. The taste was so much better. As you can imagine, such a large amount of weed kept me busy most days. My weed business became my refuge. I taught myself to be patient. Gradually, I got used to the silence from my family. How long could it last?

If my family shunned me and subjected me to forced exile from their lives, at least my illegitimate dealings did not disappoint me.

twelve

TODAY IS THE LAST DAY that we will spend together. The fifth day of my confession to you. I have brought something for you. The outdoor weed. Doesn't it smell amazing? My mother would kill me if she knew I had brought it into the house. It's her own fault that she's so ignorant about my life.

You are probably wondering how is it possible that my parents never found out what I really do? Or anybody else in the family?

I am a world-class liar. It's one of my best qualities. Never forget that.

Now, let's begin.

It was a Saturday afternoon. I was lying on the sofa, rolling a joint. The first few plants were ready. Too fresh to sell yet but I wanted to see how they tasted. I closed my eyes and let myself drift away. I don't remember why now, perhaps it was the weed that made me mellow, but I picked up the phone and dialled Krzysiek's number. I did not expect him to answer it but to my surprise he did.

'How's Alicja?' I asked.

'She went out for a walk with Marianna.'

'The girl must be big now. How old is she? Three years old?'

'We are back living together again. I mean, I moved in with her.'

'You did?'

'You sound surprised. Isn't that what you wanted?' he asked.

'Yes. I did.'

'It was me. I told her about that night. I thought you'd like to know.'

'Why did you do that?' I asked in a calm voice.

'Are you stoned again?'

'Does it matter?'

'To me it does.'

'Cut the crap. What are you now, my mother?'

'Suit yourself.'

'Why did you tell her? Did she ask you to do that? Confess your sins, repent, in order for her to grant you her forgiveness?'

'Don't be so sarcastic.'

I exhaled the smoke. 'Can't help it.'

'I wanted to come clean with her. I needed a fresh start.'

'Until you sleep with somebody else,' I said.

'No. This is it. I understand that I did the wrong thing.'

'You mean having sex with me? I thought you enjoyed the fuck. I certainly didn't hear any complaints from you. On the contrary.' I felt a surge of pitying condescension.

'Back to your old self.'

'Don't change the subject. Now you're going to be a loving and caring husband and a father. Is that what you want?'

'What do you want?'

'We are not talking about me.'

'You have some serious issues, Magda. You need to let go of that anger.'

'Oh, I'm sorry, Mr Perfect. But let me think about it. Was it me or you who invited me to your flat?'

'You could have said no.'

'You men are all the same. Moaning about an unhappy marriage, have a quick fuck in the meantime, and then run to hold your wife's skirt and wipe your nose.'

'Are you jealous?'

'About what?'

'Me and Alicja.'

'It's your life.'

'What is it then?'

'I'm upset that Alicja is not talking to me anymore. She's clearly blaming me, but not you. And you simply couldn't keep your mouth shut, could you? You had to come clean with her at my expense.' I started to roll another joint.

'It's not like that. Please, Magda, you are taking it the wrong way.'

'Am I? It's not my fault you couldn't keep your dick in your pants.'

'You can be so vulgar.'

'Whatever.'

'I guess I finally realized what's important in life.'

'That's a relief. Life is not always about you, Krzysiek. You keep forgetting that. I wanted you to go back to Alicja because I know she loves you very much and with Marianna, they both need you, but I didn't want you to tell her. I thought you would be at least clever enough to keep your mouth shut.'

'I'm sorry. I told you I had to come clean.'

'I don't give a shit whether you are sorry or not,' I exhaled the smoke. 'Alicja is my sister and I love her. She's everything to me. You broke her by telling her. If you really want to come clean, I suggest you tell her exactly what happened.'

'Or, else?'

'Or else, I will tell her. About me, about all the other women.'

'You wouldn't,' he said almost in a whisper. 'And how...'

'Watch me.'

I really don't like it when people underestimate me. Piotrek is a gifted grower. But without the lawyer I could do nothing. His contacts in the police come in handy. Which reminds me that I need to contact him about that man in the botanical gardens. Something about him wasn't right. Not that you should be worried. It's my job to protect you now.

Thank God for the bribes. It takes so little to obtain information.

I cannot begin to tell you how much I missed my sister. Alicja made everything real when nothing seemed true anymore. The harrowing emptiness without her voice and our late-night conversations was taking its toll on me. She kept me sane when I was losing my faith in what a family was. And now everything is gone. The person I have become doesn't regret betraying my sister but then she never really gave any serious thought to what Alicja would say, or anybody else. I am not saying that being a drug dealer doesn't make me proud of myself. I am. I am truly proud of what she has built throughout the years, of what she and I have achieved. Her small kingdom of addiction. Sometimes I wish she could have given more consideration to what I felt. It's too late for that now.

I could not allow myself to lose my sister.

Not again.

Yes, there is this memory I haven't told you about. How she almost killed her. I think it was then that the consciousness of the other me began slowly budding inside me. But it happened because she felt threatened that Alicja would discover her secret. It was at the time when she was establishing her cannabis contacts in the park, forging relationships that would define our life together for years to come. One day Alicja took my jacket – whether my sister began to suspect something or not is irrelevant now – and found a small bag of cannabis in the pocket. She confronted me. She said she would tell our mother if I didn't confess the whole truth about what was going on, what I was getting myself into. I made a promise that I would tell her everything the next day. But that night I could not sleep. Alicja's breath was so even as I watched her sleep, while she was already raging inside me, trying to break free, arguing with me about what right Alicja had to tell me what to do, to hold her hostage! She stood by my sister's bed, watching, her head cocked to one side, clutching a pillow in her hands. Like it was some kind of sick contest. What are you going to do now? How are you going to defend your sister? What's her life worth when yours can be so much better if you only listen to me? Me, my worst enemy, my biggest admirer. I stopped her hands and placed the pillow next to my sister's face.

I have made my choices. I live with them every day of my life.

When I got back to London after visiting my family, I settled back into my life without thinking about how to heal the breach of trust between us. I thought with time it would resolve itself, it would calm down, Alicja would calm down. And she did. She refused to talk to me, to respond to my emails, text messages, phone calls. Now I knew it was because she had taken Krzysiek in, as if to show me she was standing above what I did to her.

After the conversation with Krzysiek, I decided to ignore her silence. That Saturday I emailed her to say that I was flying to Warsaw and that I would be waiting in the café in my hotel. For the first few days after I emailed her, there was no response, then a day before my flight she texted me to say that she would come to see me.

Yes, well, I had to meet Piotrek as well, inspect the site and make plans for the spring operation. I took my chances and hoped she would see me.

I flew to Warsaw into a biting January winter. It was minus sixteen Celsius. For the first time nobody was waiting for me at the airport. I hailed one of the taxis waiting outside and went directly to the Bristol hotel. In my room I changed my clothes and went to the café downstairs. Sitting on my own, I had no idea whether she would come. It had been forty minutes already and I was on my second cappuccino and fourth cigarette. She had the perfect right to hate me and punish me with dead air for as long as she wished. But I was going nowhere until I had seen her.

'I'm sorry I'm late,' Alicja said, rushing in. I was happy to see her but she avoided my hug when I stood up.

'I'm really pleased you decided to come,' I said, sitting down.

'We can't choose our family.' Instead of looking at me she picked up the menu.

'Still.'

'Did you think I wouldn't come?' She raised her pencil thin eyebrows.

'I don't know.'

'How's work? Are you still in the same madhouse?'

'Yes.' My laughter covered my lie. I was tense.

'Do you intend to stay there? It's been, what, more than two years now. That would make our mother happy.'

'I don't know. We'll see.'

'Oh well, I guess it doesn't matter that much to you what other people think.' She sounded amused. I was not.

'It's okay.'

'Maybe you should. Think about it. But I know that eventually you'll do whatever you want. You were always like that. Never listening to others or caring what others would think about you.' She put the menu down on the table and waved at the waitress to get her attention.

'How's Marianna?' I asked.

'She's great,' Alicja smiled. 'I love her to death. Here, have a look.' Alicja took a digital camera from her handbag and showed me the photographs.

'Do you still enjoy it? You know, being a mum?' I gave her back the camera.

'Yes. But I'm getting more work now and I can take some of it home. I'm finally getting the balance right. I loved being with her, at the very beginning, but now I want to go back to full time work.'

'Yes, I remember mother mentioned that you had two nannies, which obviously pissed her off as she wanted to come to Warsaw.'

'I know. She was pretty unhappy that I didn't want her to come.' She laughed for the first time since she came. 'Sometimes I envy your freedom,' she said quietly.

I leaned forward in my chair. 'What do you mean?'

'Oh, you know, living far away from her. She can't take a train and come and visit you. Like she does with me. Don't get me wrong. I like her being around and helping with Marianna, but sometimes ...' She didn't finish the sentence. Instead she put her hand on mine and said, 'I know why you left. Despite everything that happened between us I want you to know that I understand. There was a time when I hated you, I hated what you did to me.'

There was a moment of silence between us before I said, 'I spoke to Krzysiek.'

'When?'

'He told me you are back together again.'

She nodded her head.

'Has he told you what really happened?'

'About what? That you slept with him?' She looked straight into my eyes. It was a blank stare. The moment of her fragility was gone in front of my eyes. It made me think that she would have made an excellent dealer. 'We don't talk about it. It's done.'

'There's so much I want you to know.'

You see, that was the first time I wanted to be honest with her and tell her exactly who I was. Tell her everything but I couldn't. I was a coward. I think I was afraid I would lose her forever. And that was unimaginable to me then.

'What's the point?' she interrupted me. 'You slept with him. And that's it. I don't want to go back to that. I forgave him. He's a guy. They sleep around constantly. Isn't that what you've always said?' A self-mocking smile escaped her lips.

'I think you should know he wanted it.'

'You didn't have to do it. You could have chosen not to do it, for me. Did you think about it when he was inside you? Did it actually cross your mind?'

'I don't know why I did it,' I said slowly. 'If I say for sport you will hate me even more. You are right: I didn't have to do it. But I did. But I didn't seduce him. He wanted to have sex with me. I thought you should know, before you start forgiving him.'

'I have already,' she stated.

'I'm not a bad person.'

She laughed bitterly and took a sip of her coffee. 'Of course you aren't. Nobody is. You are simply insensitive sometimes. And you know no boundaries. You hurt people around you. You know that. You hurt me and mother. You destroy everything and everybody. You destroy people who care about you. If you keep doing it there will be nobody left. Perhaps somebody should stop you from destroying yourself.'

'What do you want from me? Do you want me to apologise to everybody? Do you want me to beg for your forgiveness?' I was suddenly tired.

'I think it's beyond that now. You made your own decisions. You should have thought about the consequences. But you never do that, do you?'

I wanted to say that I was sorry. But was I really? I was not sorry about anything that had happened. Of all the people, I craved her forgiveness the most and yet I was unable to utter the words she was waiting for.

'I don't want you to send that letter about apostasy,' she said slowly.

'You know how important it is to me.'

'I realize that. But if you want me back and you want me to forgive you, then I want you to do this one thing. For me.'

'You realize what you are asking me to do?'

I knew this moment required a reiteration of loyalty to my sister, my family, my country. What she was asking me to do was to submit, for the sake of our sisterly bond. The family. Why, why did she have to ask me that?

'If that is what you want me to do,' I said reluctantly.

'Thank you.' She squeezed my hand.

I felt uneasy agreeing to this emotional blackmail. Why was it so easy for her to move on? I wanted to believe it was worth it. I was wondering how far I was prepared to go to win her back.

I wasn't in London. I understood then that Alicja belonged to Poland. There the moral code and Christian teachings are so tightly connected with every breath of each person that breaking away from it all is almost unthinkable. Nobody questions the moral values, which always come first. For Alicja, the need to protect those values was stronger than anything else. There was no middle ground between us. How could I ever tell her who I really was? And who was the bigger liar here? Me, abandoning the privilege of choice for the sake of keeping our sisterhood together, or her, for consciously blinding herself to her husband's infidelities? The thought of our inane lies to each other was almost sobering but I still engaged in this pretence of authenticity between us.

No matter how far I travelled away from Poland, there was no escape from the tentacles of self-flagellation for daring to challenge the sanctity of the moral conduct we had been brought up with. Alicja knew exactly what to demand to make me pay the highest price. It was her triumph and she knew it.

I stayed in Warsaw for one night, to finish the process of redeeming myself in the eyes of my family.

I phoned my mother. Talking to her while being physically in London seemed so surreal. It was easier to grasp the feelings of guilt while immersing myself in the culture I was trying to escape from.

'I knew Alicja was going to talk some sense into you,' my mother said with satisfaction in her voice.

'Yes, you're right,' I said.

'See, it wasn't as painful as you thought. You will thank me one day.'

'Like during my Catholic funeral?'

'Magda, that's just not nice. Not nice at all.'

'I'm sorry.' Would I have to wait for my mother to die to submit the letter of apostasy? Or for Alicja to die? I banished the thought.

'Alicja told me you are going back to London tomorrow. I thought you would at least stay for a few more days and visit us.'

'I've got to go back to work.'

'Can't you take some time off?'

'I just did, mother, to come and see Alicja.'

'Well, why don't you plan it in advance next time and come and visit us? Or we can come to see you. What do you think?'

I didn't particularly fancy going back to POSK to meet bright young Poles. My life had evolved and it was too late for me for to have the cultural awakening she craved. Besides, since I had seriously started growing weed at home, it would be tricky to have her nosy face around. Last time, my perceptive mother promptly asked, 'What's that funny odour?' and it took me a while to convince her the 'funny' smell was emitted by the herbs I grew in pots on the kitchen window, not the plants in the basement. The incident made me think that I should buy another property where my parents could stay when they visited.

'I'm pretty busy these days,' I said.

'You always are. You never have time for us. But you have time to travel around the world and go on holiday to exotic places. Alicja told me. You never tell us but we know. Why can't you come on holiday to Poland?'

'I don't like it.'

'This is your home.'

'Mother, if I missed Poland so much, I wouldn't have left in the first place. I will come to you when I can.'

'You're always getting upset with me. I'm your mother and I want the best for you. I just think you will feel much better if you come to us more often. I will cook for you. You used to like my cooking so much.'

'I will do my best.'

'Hopefully sooner rather than later. So, Alicja told me you are doing well at work.'

'I think so,' I said noncommittally, ready to finish this conversation.

'And what about men? Have you met anybody yet?'

'No.'

'Remember that ...'

'Yes I know my clock is ticking, and no, I don't want to get married, and no, I don't want to have children.'

'There is no reason for you to talk to me like that.'

'I'm sorry. I'm not trying to undermine your parental instincts but I'm a big girl now. I'm capable of taking care of myself.'

'All right, then. But don't run crying to me in ten years' time, saying that you should have listened to me.'

'It's unlikely that will happen, trust me.' And before she managed to respond I added, 'Listen, I've got to go.'

'Where?'

'I just need to go. I've got some stuff to do.'

'Well, go then.'

'Uhm.'

'Magda, you did the right thing with that letter. I am proud of you.'

'Great. Am I going to get a medal?'

'Excuse me?'

'Never mind.'

The next day I met Piotrek. He came to the Bristol Hotel. It was safer to meet in the hotel room. We needed to get ready for the outdoor season. You might think that January is too early.

Of course it is, silly. We needed to plan the timing for taking the cuttings in the container into the open air. We usually begin planting the cuttings in mid-May, or later, depending on the weather and the temperature. The climate in eastern Poland is cooler than the rest of the country. Yes, we could have bought a plot in the western part of the country but, you see, the eastern parts are less industrialised, with fewer chances for anybody to get suspicious. The land is in the middle of nowhere, surrounded by woods. It's perfect for our business. I could take you there some day, when you grow up of course. It is not a playground. A young girl like you will probably find it boring.

I think we should take a break now. What I am about to tell you changed my life and your life forever. It was the most painful day of my whole life.

thirteen

IT WAS A TUESDAY. Yes, I remember it vividly because on Saturday Piotrek sent two cars with weed. Jerome came to my house to count the money. He had already contacted the distributors and the cannabis was on its way to Manchester, Liverpool, Newcastle and Dublin.

'Right. We will have to set up a new account, offshore. I checked the sales for the past three months. Over half a million pounds,' he said. 'Are you still going to get another cover job?'

'Nah. We've been working our arses off the past year. I'm exhausted. Besides, I don't want to go back to the office circus. Enough is enough.'

I leaned in and playfully bit his lips. 'Maybe you could take some time off and we could go to Barbados? If your new girlfriend permits?' I added with a mischievous grin. I swallowed the smoke he puffed into my mouth. He handed me the spliff and I inhaled some more.

'You are my girlfriend.'

'I'm your business partner. The fuck is just for free.' I laughed, blowing clouds of smoke into his face.

You see, throughout these years we had developed a perfect set up. I knew Jerome wanted a big family. Not my thing. Well, now, looking at you, I guess I don't have a choice.

'Hold on, somebody is calling me on my mobile.' I fished out the vibrating phone from a pocket.

It was my father. I remember thinking that it was very strange, my father calling me in the middle of the night.

'I have to take this,' I said and went to the bedroom holding the phone to my chest.

'Magda,' he said, his voice trembling as if he was crying. I had never seen my father crying. Something was wrong. Something terrible had happened.

'What is it?' I asked impatiently. 'What is it? Just tell me.'

'Alicja and Krzysiek had a car accident a few hours ago. On the motorway. She died instantly. Krzysiek is in a coma at the hospital. It was a truck. Head on collision. I am calling from the hospital.' As he spoke, his words broke up and he swallowed his tears.

'And Marianna? Dad! What about Marianna?' My hands were shaking. I collapsed on the floor and leaned against the bed frame.

'She's okay. She's at the hospital but she's fine. I don't know how it's possible. Oh my God. You have to come back to Poland, Magda. You have to come back. You have to take care of Marianna. That's what Alicja always said to us, if anything happened to her.' He was sobbing, slurring his words as I tried to make sense of what was happening, and what it would mean for me and my business.

I don't remember your mother ever saying to me that if anything happened to her I would be the legal guardian to her daughter. The chances of both Alicja and Krzysiek dying were impossible to imagine. Until now.

'I will book the flight for tomorrow,' I whispered.

The phone slipped from my fingers and hit the floor.

Why had she never told me she wanted me to take care of you? Why did she have to leave it until her death for me to find out? I am so angry with her. I am so angry I am unable to cry.

the day of the funeral

I KNOW YOU ARE ONLY FIVE YEARS OLD. I know you have no idea what I have been telling you for the last five days. You look at me and you see a woman muttering to herself in two languages that you are yet to master. You don't even know who I am. Will you remember this story of my past, of her obsession, her willingness to sacrifice even her family to stay alive? For the past five days and nights I have spoken aloud words that have no real meaning for you. Not now, at least. You have been a good listener, a patient spectator of my existence, a witness to my confession.

What am I going to do with you now? Will you learn how to love me? Will I? I don't know if your dad is ever going to wake up. When I went to the hospital, the doctors told me that he has brain damage. Even if he wakes up he will be in no state to take care of you, which leaves me with no choice. It seems to me unbearably sad for life to start that way for you, with the deaths of the people who are supposed to defend you against people like me. Instead, your mother's wish was for me to take care of you. Why? I still try to comprehend her actions. But what really unnerves me is the question of whether your mother had any idea what I am? Because if she did, would she really want somebody like me to take care of her only child? If she did, what kind of mother would it make her, to ask her sister, a cannabis importer, to be responsible for her child's future? I cannot stop thinking about how much she knew about me? Whether she really had the slightest idea of what my life is like?

I know that this is not the way we both imagined it and I am not the auntie you would expect to end up with. I don't cook, I don't clean, I don't have any toys, unless you count the gun I have brought with me today because I have a feeling we might have the company at the cemetery. Let it be our secret, okay? Remember that man who took our photos at the botanical gardens? Perhaps these people will respect the fact we are going to the funeral, but you never know with them. I am done hiding. No more cover jobs. No more lies between you and me. If we are ever going to manage to make it work, we will need to learn to trust each other completely because it is our lives that we are gambling with. You will learn to lie, like I did. At least you don't have parents you will need to lie to.

I can hear my mother's voice urging me to take you downstairs. Now, give me your hand. Good girl. It's time to say goodbye to your mum.

acknowledgements

THIS BOOK WOULD HAVE never been published without *Nancy Roberts*, my friend and soul sister, who makes my dreams come true and pushes me into the unknown. I owe Nancy my enormous gratitude for everything this novel has become, as well as for the third person and buckets of champagne.

I was very fortunate to have a wonderful editor, *Hywel Evans*, who infused me with excitement and whose criticism made this book so much better, seeing many things that did not occur to me. If there are any mistakes it is only my own stubborn nature in refusing to kill my darlings.

For forcing me to write the stories I only told in the clouds of cigarette smoke I owe my hearty thanks to the author, *Deon Meyer*.

When I began to write this story, having no idea what to expect, I was in a middle of my PhD studies with a full time job. Despite the fact I spent more and more time writing fiction rather than my thesis I have received nothing but support and encouragement from my colleagues and friends in academia. My deepest gratitude goes out to the best supervisor any PhD student can wish for, *Dr Ranka Primorac* for believing in me, understanding and supporting me when I broke the news about the novel. To *Dr Chris Warnes* for the Cambridge experience and everything South African. To *Dr Christine O'Dowd Smyth* for her patience with me.

My friends have always been there for me when I needed them. When I did not have time to answer phone calls or emails because I was writing they never complained. *Ole Birk Laursen, Jackie Jordan, Terri Mulholland, Kone Ndlovu* and *Mohammed Umar* for your energy and extraordinary belief that I should write. *Maria Conroy* for being the third musketeer. *Helen Fost* for touching the stars. *Marcus Graham* for political correctness. *Kamila Tomaszewska* for not reading the drafts so we could talk about everything else to keep me sane. *Matt Wells* and *Nathan Johnson* who gave me inspiration and almost never complained when I threw them out of the house on many occasions.

For surprising myself and doing it I owe my very special thanks to *Magnus Gundersen*. Without Magnus parts of this book would be incredibly boring.

I would like to mention two books which have greatly influenced *Madame Mephisto*; Misha Glenny's *McMafia, Crime Without Frontiers*, and Jack Herer's *The Emperor Wears No Clothes, Overview of the History of Cannabis Hemp*.

There are others who for obvious reasons I cannot name here. I am indebted to those who will remain anonymous for showing me a piece of a different world.

This book is dedicated to my family. Mama i tato - za to, że mnie tak mocno kochacie i wierzycie we mnie. Ta książka jest dla was. To my love, Asher Johnson, whose honesty, unfaltering support, refreshing criticism influences everything that I create. I could not write without you.

about the author

A.M. BAKALAR was born and raised in Poland. She lived in Germany, France, Sicily and Canada before she moved to the UK in 2004. *Madame Mephisto* is her first novel. A.M. Bakalar lives with her partner, a drum and bass musician, in London. She is currently at work on her second novel.

reading group guide

How important is our profession to our sense of identity? Would you say that your job defines who you are? Can you imagine what it would be like if you were involved in a criminal activity? As far as one's family is concerned, what choices do you think a person has to make if involved in crime?

Why do you think Magda is trying to escape from her family? Is it because she wants to protect her family, or is it because she is a cold-blooded criminal? How much is Magda sacrificing herself to get what she wants? Is it worth it?

What is the nature of the relationship Magda has with her mother and how does it affect her decisions? Why do you think she keeps lying to her mother?

Magda's mother and her twin sister Alicja are strong female characters. What do you think they think of Magda? Do you think they understand what Magda is doing and choose to ignore it?

As the story progresses Magda's alter-ego becomes more and more visible. How much of Magda's choices are hers and how much are they of the persona she creates? Do you think Magda has a split personality, or does she simply choose to behave in a certain way, depending on the situation? Does Magda know who she really is?

Consider the strengths and weaknesses of the novel. Is the narrator reliable? What about the structure of the narrative? Is Magda's monologue compelling?

Magda has a number of relationships with men and often uses sex to get what she wants. Is her behaviour moral?

At the beginning of the novel Magda says: 'This family! It's so much easier to love each other from a distance.' Do you agree with this statement? How much does our family influence the choices we make in life? Is it ever possible to run away from your own family?

Discuss the theme of immigration. What does it mean for a person to live in another country? How much you think a person changes to fit in into a new society? Magda's mother says: 'Your family and your home are here. You are a foreigner there and you will always be.' Do you agree?

Language plays a key role in the novel. Magda is criticised in both societies for the way she speaks. How much does language influence perceptions of Magda among the British and the Poles?

Did you like the ending? Do you think the person Magda has been telling her story to will come back to London with her? Do you think Magda is the right person to take on responsibility for somebody else?

forthcoming titles from stork press

Illegal Liaisons by Grażyna Plebanek
Publication date: October 2012
Translator: Danusia Stok
ISBN Paperback: 978-0-9571326-2-7
ISBN eBook: 978-0-9571326-3-4

Freshta by Petra Procházková
Publication date: October 2012
Translator: Julia Sherwood
ISBN Paperback: 978-0-9571326-4-1
ISBN eBook: 978-0-9571326-5-8

The Finno-Ugrian Vampire by Noémi Szécsi
Publication date: October 2012
Translator: Peter Sherwood
ISBN Paperback: 978-0-9571326-6-5
ISBN eBook: 978-0-9571326-7-2